OF $ 1 50

WITHDRAWN

THE DOCTOR'S DILEMMA

Jennifer Dubedat
Katharine Cornell

THE DOCTOR'S DILEMMA

With Preface on Doctors

By

BERNARD SHAW

WITH ILLUSTRATIONS FROM
THE PLAY AS PRESENTED BY
KATHARINE CORNELL

Dodd, Mead & Company

NEW YORK · 1941

PRINTED IN THE UNITED STATES OF AMERICA
BY THE VAIL-BALLOU PRESS, INC., BINGHAMTON, N. Y.

24963

CONTENTS

v

CONTENTS

ILLUSTRATIONS

Katharine Cornell's production of "The Doctor's Dilemma," directed by Guthrie McClintic, beginning March 11th., 1941, at the Shubert Theatre, New York, with this cast:

Redpenny . . . . STANLEY BELL

Emmy . . . . ALICE BELMORE CLIFFE

Sir Colenso Ridgeon . . . . RAYMOND MASSEY

Dr. Schutzmacher . . . . CLARENCE DERWENT

Sir Patrick Cullen . . . . WHITFORD KANE

Mr. Cutler Walpole . . . . RALPH FORBES

Sir Ralph Bloomfield Bonington . . . . . CECIL HUMPHREYS

Dr. Blenkinsop . . . . COLIN KEITH-JOHNSTON

Jennifer Dubedat . . . . KATHARINE CORNELL

Louis Dubedat . . . . BRAMWELL FLETCHER

Minnie Tinwell . . . . MARGARET CURTIS

The Newspaper Man . . . . LESLIE BARRIE

A Secretary . . . . DAVID ORRICK

PREFACE ON DOCTORS

IT is not the fault of our doctors that the medical service of the community, as at present provided for, is a murderous absurdity. That any sane nation, having observed that you could provide for the supply of bread by giving bakers a pecuniary interest in baking for you, should go on to give a surgeon a pecuniary interest in cutting off your leg, is enough to make one despair of political humanity. But that is precisely what we have done. And the more appalling the mutilation, the more the mutilator is paid. He who corrects the ingrowing toe-nail receives a few shillings: he who cuts your inside out receives hundreds of guineas, except when he does it to a poor person for practice.

Scandalized voices murmur that these operations are necessary. They may be. It may also be necessary to hang a man or pull down a house. But we take good care not to make the hangman and the housebreaker the judges of that. If we did, no man's neck would be safe and no man's house stable. But we do make the doctor the judge, and fine him anything from sixpence to several hundred guineas if he decides in our favor. I cannot knock my shins severely without forcing on some surgeon the difficult question, "Could I not make a better use of a pocketful of guineas than this man is making of his leg? Could he not write as well—or even better—on one leg than on two? And the guineas would make all the difference in the world to me just now. My wife—my pretty ones—the leg may mortify—it is always safer to operate—he will be well in a fortnight—artificial legs are now so well made that they are really better than natural ones—evolution is towards motors and leglessness, &c., &c., &c."

Now there is no calculation that an engineer can make as to the behavior of a girder under a strain, or an astronomer as to the recurrence of a comet, more certain than the calculation that under such circumstances we shall be dismembered unnecessarily in all directions by surgeons who believe the operations to be necessary solely because they want

I

to perform them. The process metaphorically called bleeding the rich man is performed not only metaphorically but literally every day by surgeons who are quite as honest as most of us. After all, what harm is there in it? The surgeon need not take off the rich man's (or woman's) leg or arm: he can remove the appendix or the uvula, and leave the patient none the worse after a fortnight or so in bed, whilst the nurse, the general practitioner, the apothecary, and the surgeon will be the better.

DOUBTFUL CHARACTER BORNE BY THE MEDICAL PROFESSION

Again I hear the voices indignantly muttering old phrases about the high character of a noble profession and the honor and conscience of its members. I must reply that the medical profession has not a high character; it has an infamous character. I do not know a single thoughtful and well-informed person who does not feel that the tragedy of illness at present is that it delivers you helplessly into the hands of a profession which you deeply mistrust, because it not only advocates and practises the most revolting cruelties in the pursuit of knowledge, and justifies them on grounds which would equally justify practising the same cruelties on yourself or your children, or burning down London to test a patent fire extinguisher, but, when it has shocked the public, tries to reassure it with lies of breath-bereaving brazenness. That is the character the medical profession has got just now. It may be deserved or it may not: there it is at all events, and the doctors who have not realized this are living in a fool's paradise. As to the honor and conscience of doctors, they have as much as any other class of men, no more and no less. And what other men dare pretend to be impartial where they have a strong pecuniary interest on one side? Nobody supposes that doctors are less virtuous than judges; but a judge whose salary and reputation depended on whether the verdict was for plaintiff or defendant, prosecutor or prisoner, would be as little trusted as a general in the pay of the enemy. To offer me a doctor as

PREFACE ON DOCTORS

my judge, and then weight his decision with a bribe of a large sum of money and a virtual guarantee that if he makes a mistake it can never be proved against him, is to go wildly beyond the ascertained strain which human nature will bear. It is simply unscientific to allege or believe that doctors do not under existing circumstances perform unnecessary operations and manufacture and prolong lucrative illnesses. The only ones who can claim to be above suspicion are those who are so much sought after that their cured patients are immediately replaced by fresh ones. And there is this curious psychological fact to be remembered: a serious illness or a death advertizes the doctor exactly as a hanging advertizes the barrister who defended the person hanged. Suppose, for example, a royal personage gets something wrong with his throat, or has a pain in his inside. If a doctor effects some trumpery cure with a wet compress or a peppermint lozenge nobody takes the least notice of him. But if he operates on the throat and kills the patient, or extirpates an internal organ and keeps the whole nation palpitating for days whilst the patient hovers in pain and fever between life and death, his fortune is made: every rich man who omits to call him in when the same symptoms appear in his household is held not to have done his utmost duty to the patient. The wonder is that there is a king or queen left alive in Europe.

DOCTORS' CONSCIENCES

There is another difficulty in trusting to the honor and conscience of a doctor. Doctors are just like other Englishmen: most of them have no honor and no conscience: what they commonly mistake for these is sentimentality and an intense dread of doing anything that everybody else does not do, or omitting to do anything that everybody else does. This of course does amount to a sort of working or rule-of-thumb conscience; but it means that you will do anything, good or bad, provided you get enough people to keep you in countenance by doing it also. It is the sort of conscience that makes it possible to keep order on a pirate

3

PREFACE ON DOCTORS

ship, or in a troop of brigands. It may be said that in the last analysis there is no other sort of honor or conscience in existence—that the assent of the majority is the only sanction known to ethics. No doubt this holds good in political practice. If mankind knew the facts, and agreed with the doctors, then the doctors would be in the right; and any person who thought otherwise would be a lunatic. But mankind does not agree, and does not know the facts. All that can be said for medical popularity is that until there is a practicable alternative to blind trust in the doctor, the truth about the doctor is so terrible that we dare not face it. Molière saw through the doctors; but he had to call them in just the same. Napoleon had no illusions about them; but he had to die under their treatment just as much as the most credulous ignoramus that ever paid sixpence for a bottle of strong medicine. In this predicament most people, to save themselves from unbearable mistrust and misery, or from being driven by their conscience into actual conflict with the law, fall back on the old rule that if you cannot have what you believe in you must believe in what you have. When your child is ill or your wife dying, and you happen to be very fond of them, or even when, if you are not fond of them, you are human enough to forget every personal grudge before the spectacle of a fellow creature in pain or peril, what you want is comfort, reassurance, something to clutch at, were it but a straw. This the doctor brings you. You have a wildly urgent feeling that something must be done; and the doctor does something. Sometimes what he does kills the patient; but you do not know that; and the doctor assures you that all that human skill could do has been done. And nobody has the brutality to say to the newly bereft father, mother, husband, wife, brother, or sister, "You have killed your lost darling by your credulity."

THE PECULIAR PEOPLE

Besides, the calling in of the doctor is now compulsory except in cases where the patient is an adult and not too ill to decide the steps to be taken. We are subject to prosecu-

4

tion for manslaughter or for criminal neglect if the patient dies without the consolations of the medical profession. This menace is kept before the public by the Peculiar People. The Peculiars, as they are called, have gained their name by believing that the Bible is infallible, and taking their belief quite seriously. The Bible is very clear as to the treatment of illness. The Epistle of James, chapter v., contains the following explicit directions:—

14. Is any sick among you? let him call for the elders of the Church; and let them pray over him, anointing him with oil in the name of the Lord:

15. And the prayer of faith shall save the sick, and the Lord shall raise him up; and if he have committed sins, they shall be forgiven him.

The Peculiars obey these instructions and dispense with doctors. They are therefore prosecuted for manslaughter when their children die.

When I was a young man, the Peculiars were usually acquitted. The prosecution broke down when the doctor in the witness box was asked whether, if the child had had medical attendance, it would have lived. It was, of course, impossible for any man of sense and honor to assume divine omniscience by answering this in the affirmative, or indeed pretending to be able to answer it at all. And on this the judge had to instruct the jury that they must acquit the prisoner. Thus a judge with a keen sense of law (a very rare phenomenon on the Bench, by the way) was spared the possibility of having to sentence one prisoner (under the Blasphemy Laws) for questioning the authority of Scripture, and another for ignorantly and superstitiously accepting it as a guide to conduct. Today all this is changed. The doctor never hesitates to claim divine omniscience, nor to clamor for laws to punish any scepticism on the part of laymen. A modern doctor thinks nothing of signing the death certificate of one of his own diphtheria patients, and then going into the witness box and swearing a Peculiar into prison for six months by assuring the jury, on oath, that

5

if the prisoner's child, dead of diphtheria, had been placed under his treatment instead of that of St James, it would not have died. And he does so not only with impunity, but with public applause, though the logical course would be to prosecute him either for the murder of his own patient, or for perjury in the case of St James. Yet no barrister, apparently, dreams of asking for the statistics of the relative case-mortality in diphtheria among the Peculiars and among the believers in doctors, on which alone any valid opinion could be founded. The barrister is as superstitious as the doctor is infatuated; and the Peculiar goes unpitied to his cell, though nothing whatever has been proved except that his child died without the interference of a doctor as effectually as any of the hundreds of children who die every day of the same diseases in the doctor's care.

RECOIL OF THE DOGMA OF MEDICAL INFALLIBILITY ON THE DOCTOR

On the other hand, when the doctor is in the dock, or is the defendant in an action for malpractice, he has to struggle against the inevitable result of his former pretences to infinite knowledge and unerring skill. He has taught the jury and the judge, and even his own counsel, to believe that every doctor can, with a glance at the tongue, a touch on the pulse, and a reading of the clinical thermometer, diagnose with absolute certainty a patient's complaint, also that on dissecting a dead body he can infallibly put his finger on the cause of death, and, in cases where poisoning is suspected, the nature of the poison used. Now all this supposed exactness and infallibility is imaginary; and to treat a doctor as if his mistakes were necessarily malicious or corrupt malpractices (an inevitable deduction from the postulate that the doctor, being omniscient, cannot make mistakes) is as unjust as to blame the nearest apothecary for not being prepared to supply you with sixpenny-worth of the elixir of life, or the nearest motor garage for not having perpetual motion on sale in gallon tins. But if apothecaries and motor car makers habitually advertized elixir of life and perpetual motion, and succeeded in creating a strong general belief that they could supply it, they would find themselves in an awkward position if they were indicted for allowing a customer to die, or for burning a chauffeur by putting petrol into his car. That is the predicament the doctor finds himself in when he has to defend himself against a charge of malpractice by a plea of ignorance and fallibility. His plea is received with flat incredulity; and he gets little sympathy, even from laymen who know, because he has brought the incredulity on himself. If he escapes, he can only do so by opening the eyes of the jury to the facts that medical science is as yet very imperfectly differentiated from common curemongering witchcraft; that diagnosis, though it means in many instances (including even the identification of pathogenic bacilli under the miscroscope) only a choice among terms so loose that they would not be accepted as definitions in any really exact science, is, even at that, an uncertain and difficult matter on which doctors often differ; and that the very best medical opinion and treatment varies widely from doctor to doctor, one practitioner prescribing six or seven scheduled poisons for so familiar a disease as enteric fever where another will not tolerate drugs at all; one starving a patient whom another would stuff; one urging an operation which another would regard as unnecessary and dangerous; one giving alcohol and meat which another would sternly forbid, &c., &c., &c.: all these discrepancies arising not between the opinion of good doctors and bad ones (the medical contention is, of course, that a bad doctor is an impossibility), but between practitioners of equal eminence and authority. Usually it is impossible to persuade the jury that these facts are facts. Juries seldom notice facts; and they have been taught to regard any doubts of the omniscience and omnipotence of doctors as blasphemy. Even the fact that doctors themselves die of the very diseases they profess to cure passes unnoticed. We do not shoot out our lips and shake our heads, saying, "They save others: themselves they cannot save":

7

their reputation stands, like an African king's palace, on a foundation of dead bodies; and the result is that the verdict goes against the defendant when the defendant is a doctor accused of malpractice.

Fortunately for the doctors, they very seldom find themselves in this position, because it is so difficult to prove anything against them. The only evidence that can decide a case of malpractice is expert evidence: that is, the evidence of other doctors; and every doctor will allow a colleague to decimate a whole countryside sooner than violate the bond of professional etiquet by giving him away. It is the nurse who gives the doctor away in private, because every nurse has some particular doctor whom she likes; and she usually assures her patients that all the others are disastrous noodles, and soothes the tedium of the sick-bed by gossip about their blunders. She will even give a doctor away for the sake of making the patient believe that she knows more than the doctor. But she dare not, for her livelihood, give the doctor away in public. And the doctors stand by one another at all costs. Now and then some doctor in an unassailable position, like the late Sir William Gull, will go into the witness box and say what he really thinks about the way a patient has been treated; but such behavior is considered little short of infamous by his colleagues.

WHY DOCTORS DO NOT DIFFER

The truth is, there would never be any public agreement among doctors if they did not agree to agree on the main point of the doctor being always in the right. Yet the two guinea man never thinks that the five shilling man is right: if he did, he would be understood as confessing to an over-charge of £1:17s.; and on the same ground the five shilling man cannot encourage the notion that the owner of the six-penny surgery round the corner is quite up to his mark. Thus even the layman has to be taught that infallibility is not quite infallible, because there are two qualities of it to be had at two prices.

But there is no agreement even in the same rank at the

PREFACE ON DOCTORS

same price. During the first great epidemic of influenza towards the end of the nineteenth century a London evening paper sent round a journalist-patient to all the great consultants of that day, and published their advice and prescriptions: a proceeding passionately denounced by the medical papers as a breach of confidence of these eminent physicians. The case was the same; but the prescriptions were different, and so was the advice. Now a doctor cannot think his own treatment right and at the same time think his colleague right in prescribing a different treatment when the patient is the same. Anyone who has ever known doctors well enough to hear medical shop talked without reserve knows that they are full of stories about each other's blunders and errors, and that the theory of their omniscience and omnipotence no more holds good among themselves than it did with Molière and Napoleon. But for this very reason no doctor dare accuse another of malpractice. He is not sure enough of his own opinion to ruin another man by it. He knows that if such conduct were tolerated in his profession no doctor's livelihood or reputation would be worth a year's purchase. I do not blame him: I should do the same myself. But the effect of this state of things is to make the medical profession a conspiracy to hide its own shortcomings. No doubt the same may be said of all professions. They are all conspiracies against the laity; and I do not suggest that the medical conspiracy is either better or worse than the military conspiracy, the legal conspiracy, the sacerdotal conspiracy, the pedagogic conspiracy, the royal and aristocratic conspiracy, the literary and artistic conspiracy, and the innumerable industrial, commercial, and financial conspiracies, from the trade unions to the great exchanges, which make up the huge conflict which we call society. But it is less suspected. The Radicals who used to advocate, as an indispensable preliminary to social reform, the strangling of the last king with the entrails of the last priest, substituted compulsory vaccination for compulsory baptism without a murmur.

9

THE CRAZE FOR OPERATIONS

Thus everything is on the side of the doctor. When men die of disease they are said to die from natural causes. When they recover (and they mostly do) the doctor gets the credit of curing them. In surgery all operations are recorded as successful if the patient can be got out of the hospital or nursing home alive, though the subsequent history of the case may be such as would make an honest surgeon vow never to recommend or perform the operation again. The large range of operations which consist of amputating limbs and extirpating organs admits of no direct verification of their necessity. There is a fashion in operations as there is in sleeves and skirts: the triumph of some surgeon who has at last found out how to make a once desperate operation fairly safe is usually followed by a rage for that operation not only among the doctors, but actually among their patients. There are men and women whom the operating table seems to fascinate: half-alive people who through vanity, or hypochondria, or a craving to be the constant objects of anxious attention or what not, lose such feeble sense as they ever had of the value of their own organs and limbs. They seem to care as little for mutilation as lobsters or lizards, which at least have the excuse that they grow new claws and new tails if they lose the old ones. Whilst this book was being prepared for the press a case was tried in the Courts, of a man who sued a railway company for damages because a train had run over him and amputated both his legs. He lost his case because it was proved that he had deliberately contrived the occurrence himself for the sake of getting an idler's pension at the expense of the railway company, being too dull to realize how much more he had to lose than to gain by the bargain even if he had won his case and received damages above his utmost hopes.

This amazing case makes it possible to say, with some prospect of being believed, that there is in the classes who can afford to pay for fashionable operations a sprinkling of

10

persons so incapable of appreciating the relative importance of preserving their bodily integrity (including the capacity for parentage) and the pleasure of talking about themselves and hearing themselves talked about as the heroes and heroines of sensational operations, that they tempt surgeons to operate on them not only with huge fees, but with personal solicitation. Now it cannot be too often repeated that when an operation is once performed, nobody can ever prove that it was unnecessary. If I refuse to allow my leg to be amputated, its mortification and my death may prove that I was wrong; but if I let the leg go, nobody can ever prove that it would not have mortified had I been obstinate. Operation is therefore the safe side for the surgeon as well as the lucrative side. The result is that we hear of "conservative surgeons" as a distinct class of practitioners who make it a rule not to operate if they can possibly help it, and who are sought after by the people who have vitality enough to regard an operation as a last resort. But no surgeon is bound to take the conservative view. If he believes that an organ is at best a useless survival, and that if he extirpates it the patient will be well and none the worse in a fortnight, whereas to await the natural cure would mean a month's illness, then he is clearly justified in recommending the operation even if the cure without operation is as certain as anything of the kind ever can be. Thus the conservative surgeon and the radical or extirpatory surgeon may both be right as far as the ultimate cure is concerned; so that their consciences do not help them out of their differences.

CREDULITY AND CHLOROFORM

There is no harder scientific fact in the world than the fact that belief can be produced in practically unlimited quantity and intensity, without observation or reasoning, and even in defiance of both, by the simple desire to believe founded on a strong interest in believing. Everybody recognizes this in the case of the amatory infatuations of the adolescents who see angels and heroes in obviously (to others) commonplace and even objectionable maidens and

PREFACE ON DOCTORS

youths. But it holds good over the entire field of human activity. The hardest-headed materialist will become a consulter of table-rappers and slate-writers if he loses a child or a wife so beloved that the desire to revive and communicate with them becomes irresistible. The cobbler believes that there is nothing like leather. The Imperialist who regards the conquest of England by a foreign power as the worst of political misfortunes believes that the conquest of a foreign power by England would be a boon to the conquered. Doctors are no more proof against such illusions than other men. Can anyone then doubt that under existing conditions a great deal of unnecessary and mischievous operating is bound to go on, and that patients are encouraged to imagine that modern surgery and anesthesia have made operations much less serious matters than they really are? When doctors write or speak to the public about operations, they imply, and often say in so many words, that chloroform has made surgery painless. People who have been operated on know better. The patient does not feel the knife, and the operation is therefore enormously facilitated for the surgeon; but the patient pays for the anesthesia with hours of wretched sickness; and when that is over there is the pain of the wound made by the surgeon, which has to heal like any other wound. This is why operating surgeons, who are usually out of the house with their fee in their pockets before the patient has recovered consciousness, and who therefore see nothing of the suffering witnessed by the general practitioner and the nurse, occasionally talk of operations very much as the hangman in Barnaby Rudge talked of executions, as if being operated on were a luxury in sensation as well as in price.

MEDICAL POVERTY

To make matters worse, doctors are hideously poor. The Irish gentleman doctor of my boyhood, who took nothing less than a guinea, though he might pay you four visits for it, seems to have no equivalent nowadays in English society. Better be a railway porter than an ordinary

12

English general practitioner. A railway porter has from eighteen to twenty-three shillings a week from the Company merely as a retainer; and his additional fees from the public, if we leave the third-class twopenny tip out of account (and I am by no means sure that even this reservation need be made), are equivalent to doctor's fees in the case of second-class passengers, and double doctor's fees in the case of first. Any class of educated men thus treated tends to become a brigand class, and doctors are no exception to the rule. They are offered disgraceful prices for advice and medicine. Their patients are for the most part so poor and so ignorant that good advice would be resented as impracticable and wounding. When you are so poor that you cannot afford to refuse eighteenpence from a man who is too poor to pay you any more, it is useless to tell him that what he or his sick child needs is not medicine, but more leisure, better clothes, better food, and a better drained and ventilated house. It is kinder to give him a bottle of something almost as cheap as water, and tell him to come again with another eighteenpence if it does not cure him. When you have done that over and over again every day for a week, how much scientific conscience have you left? If you are weak-minded enough to cling desperately to your eighteenpence as denoting a certain social superiority to the sixpenny doctor, you will be miserably poor all your life; whilst the sixpenny doctor, with his low prices and quick turnover of patients, visibly makes much more than you do and kills no more people.

A doctor's character can no more stand out against such conditions than the lungs of his patients can stand out against bad ventilation. The only way in which he can preserve his self-respect is by forgetting all he ever learnt of science, and clinging to such help as he can give without cost merely by being less ignorant and more accustomed to sick-beds than his patients. Finally, he acquires a certain skill at nursing cases under poverty-stricken domestic conditions, just as women who have been trained as domestic servants in some huge institution with lifts, vacuum cleaners, electric lighting, steam heating, and machinery that turns the kitchen into a laboratory and engine house combined, manage, when they are sent out into the world to drudge as general servants, to pick up their business in a new way, learning the slatternly habits and wretched makeshifts of homes where even bundles of kindling wood are luxuries to be anxiously economized.

THE SUCCESSFUL DOCTOR

The doctor whose success blinds public opinion to medical poverty is almost as completely demoralized. His promotion means that his practice becomes more and more confined to the idle rich. The proper advice for most of their ailments is typified in Abernethy's "Live on sixpence a day and earn it." But here, as at the other end of the scale, the right advice is neither agreeable nor practicable. And every hypochondriacal rich lady or gentleman who can be persuaded that he or she is a lifelong invalid means anything from fifty to five hundred pounds a year for the doctor. Operations enable a surgeon to earn similar sums in a couple of hours; and if the surgeon also keeps a nursing home, he may make considerable profits at the same time by running what is the most expensive kind of hotel. These gains are so great that they undo much of the moral advantage which the absence of grinding pecuniary anxiety gives the rich doctor over the poor one. It is true that the temptation to prescribe a sham treatment because the real treatment is too dear for either patient or doctor does not exist for the rich doctor. He always has plenty of genuine cases which can afford genuine treatment; and these provide him with enough sincere scientific professional work to save him from the ignorance, obsolescence, and atrophy of scientific conscience into which his poorer colleagues sink. But on the other hand his expenses are enormous. Even as a bachelor, he must, at London west end rates, make over a thousand a year before he can afford even to insure his life. His house, his servants, and his equipage (or autopage) must be on the scale to which his patients are accustomed, though a couple of rooms with a camp bed in one of them might satisfy his own requirements. Above all, the income which provides for these outgoings stops the moment he himself stops working. Unlike the man of business, whose managers, clerks, warehousemen and laborers keep his business going whilst he is in bed or in his club, the doctor cannot earn a farthing by deputy. Though he is exceptionally exposed to infection, and has to face all weathers at all hours of the night and day, often not enjoying a complete night's rest for a week, the money stops coming in the moment he stops going out; and therefore illness has special terrors for him, and success no certain permanence. He dare not stop making hay while the sun shines; for it may set at any time. Men do not resist pressure of this intensity. When they come under it as doctors they pay unnecessary visits; they write prescriptions that are as absurd as the rub of chalk with which an Irish tailor once charmed away a wart from my father's finger; they conspire with surgeons to promote operations; they nurse the delusions of the *malade imaginaire* (who is always really ill because, as there is no such thing as perfect health, nobody is ever really well); they exploit human folly, vanity, and fear of death as ruthlessly as their own health, strength, and patience are exploited by selfish hypochondriacs. They must do all these things or else run pecuniary risks that no man can fairly be asked to run. And the healthier the world becomes, the more they are compelled to live by imposture and the less by that really helpful activity of which all doctors get enough to preserve them from utter corruption. For even the most hardened humbug who ever prescribed ether tonics to ladies whose need for tonics is of precisely the same character as the need of poorer women for a glass of gin, has to help a mother through child-bearing often enough to feel that he is not living wholly in vain.

PREFACE ON DOCTORS
THE PSYCHOLOGY OF SELF-RESPECT IN SURGEONS

The surgeon, though often more unscrupulous than the general practitioner, retains his self-respect more easily. The human conscience can subsist on very questionable food. No man who is occupied in doing a very difficult thing, and doing it very well, ever loses his self-respect. The shirk, the duffer, the malingerer, the coward, the weakling, may be put out of countenance by his own failures and frauds; but the man who does evil skilfully, energetically, masterfully, grows prouder and bolder at every crime. The common man may have to found his self-respect on sobriety, honesty and industry; but a Napoleon needs no such props for his sense of dignity. If Nelson's conscience whispered to him at all in the silent watches of the night, you may depend on it it whispered about the Baltic and the Nile and Cape St Vincent, and not about his unfaithfulness to his wife. A man who robs little children when no one is looking can hardly have much self-respect or even self-esteem; but an accomplished burglar must be proud of himself. In the play to which I am at present preluding I have represented an artist who is so entirely satisfied with his artistic conscience, even to the point of dying like a saint with its support, that he is utterly selfish and unscrupulous in every other relation without feeling at the smallest disadvantage. The same thing may be observed in women who have a genius for personal attractiveness: they expend more thought, labor, skill, inventiveness, taste and endurance on making themselves lovely than would suffice to keep a dozen ugly women honest; and this enables them to maintain a high opinion of themselves, and an angry contempt for unattractive and personally careless women, whilst they lie and cheat and slander and sell themselves without a blush. The truth is, hardly any of us have ethical energy enough for more than one really inflexible point of honor. Andrea del Sarto, like Louis Dubedat in my play, must have expended on the attainment of his great mastery of

16

PREFACE ON DOCTORS

design and his originality in fresco painting more conscientiousness and industry than go to the making of the reputations of a dozen ordinary mayors and churchwardens; but (if Vasari is to be believed) when the King of France entrusted him with money to buy pictures for him, he stole it to spend on his wife. Such cases are not confined to eminent artists. Unsuccessful, unskilful men are often much more scrupulous than successful ones. In the ranks of ordinary skilled labor many men are to be found who earn good wages and are never out of a job because they are strong, indefatigable, and skilful, and who therefore are bold in a high opinion of themselves; but they are selfish and tyrannical, gluttonous and drunken, as their wives and children know to their cost.

Not only do these talented energetic people retain their self-respect through shameful misconduct: they do not even lose the respect of others, because their talents benefit and interest everybody, whilst their vices affect only a few. An actor, a painter, a composer, an author, may be as selfish as he likes without reproach from the public if only his art is superb; and he cannot fulfil this condition without sufficient effort and sacrifice to make him feel noble and martyred in spite of his selfishness. It may even happen that the selfishness of an artist may be a benefit to the public by enabling him to concentrate himself on their gratification with a recklessness of every other consideration that makes him highly dangerous to those about him. In sacrificing others to himself he is sacrificing them to the public he gratifies; and the public is quite content with that arrangement. The public actually has an interest in the artist's vices.

It has no such interest in the surgeon's vices. The surgeon's art is exercised at its expense, not for its gratification. We do not go to the operating table as we go to the theatre, to the picture gallery, to the concert room, to be entertained and delighted: we go to be tormented and maimed lest a worse thing should befall us. It is of the most extreme importance to us that the experts on whose assurance we face

17

this horror and suffer this mutilation should have no interests but our own to think of; should judge our cases scientifically; and should feel about them kindly. Let us see what guarantees we have: first for the science, and then for the kindness.

ARE DOCTORS MEN OF SCIENCE?

I presume nobody will question the existence of a widely spread popular delusion that every doctor is a man of science. It is escaped only in the very small class which understands by science something more than conjuring with retorts and spirit lamps, magnets and microscopes, and discovering magical cures for disease. To a sufficiently ignorant man every captain of a trading schooner is a Galileo, every organ-grinder a Beethoven, every piano-tuner a Helmholtz, every Old Bailey barrister a Solon, every Seven Dials pigeon-dealer a Darwin, every scrivener a Shakespear, every locomotive engine a miracle, and its driver no less wonderful than George Stephenson. As a matter of fact, the rank and file of doctors are no more scientific than their tailors; or, if you prefer to put it the reverse way, their tailors are no less scientific than they. Doctoring is an art, not a science: any layman who is interested in science sufficiently to take in one of the scientific journals and follow the literature of the scientific movement, knows more about it than those doctors (probably a large majority) who are not interested in it, and practise only to earn their bread. Doctoring is not even the art of keeping people in health (no doctor seems able to advise you what to eat any better than his grandmother or the nearest quack): it is the art of curing illnesses. It does happen exceptionally that a practising doctor makes a contribution to science (my play describes a very notable one); but it happens much oftener that he draws disastrous conclusions from his clinical experience because he has no conception of scientific method, and believes, like any rustic, that the handling of evidence and statistics needs no expertness. The distinction between a quack doctor and a qualified one is mainly that

18

only the qualified one is authorized to sign death certificates, for which both sorts seem to have about equal occasion. Unqualified practitioners now make large incomes as hygienists, and are resorted to as frequently by cultivated amateur scientists who understand quite well what they are doing as by ignorant people who are simply dupes. Bonesetters make fortunes under the very noses of our greatest surgeons from educated and wealthy patients; and some of the most successful doctors on the register use quite heretical methods of treating disease, and have qualified themselves solely for convenience. Leaving out of account the village witches who prescribe spells and sell charms, the humblest professional healers in this country are the herbalists. These men wander through the fields on Sunday seeking for herbs with magic properties of curing disease, preventing childbirth, and the like. Each of them believes that he is on the verge of a great discovery, in which Virginia Snake Root will be an ingredient, heaven knows why! Virginia Snake Root fascinates the imagination of the herbalist as mercury used to fascinate the alchemists. On week days he keeps a shop in which he sells packets of pennyroyal, dandelion, &c., labelled with little lists of the diseases they are supposed to cure, and apparently do cure to the satisfaction of the people who keep on buying them. I have never been able to perceive any distinction between the science of the herbalist and that of the duly registered doctor. A relative of mine recently consulted a doctor about some of the ordinary symptoms which indicate the need for a holiday and a change. The doctor satisfied himself that the patient's heart was a little depressed. Digitalis being a drug labelled as a heart specific by the profession, he promptly administered a stiff dose. Fortunately the patient was a hardy old lady who was not easily killed. She recovered with no worse result than her conversion to Christian Science, which owes its vogue quite as much to public despair of doctors as to superstition. I am not, observe, here concerned with the question as to whether the dose of digitalis

PREFACE ON DOCTORS

was judicious or not: the point is, that a farm laborer consulting a herbalist would have been treated in exactly the same way.

BACTERIOLOGY AS A SUPERSTITION

The smattering of science that all—even doctors—pick up from the ordinary newspapers nowadays only makes the doctor more dangerous than he used to be. Wise men used to take care to consult doctors qualified before 1860, who were usually contemptuous of or indifferent to the germ theory and bacteriological therapeutics; but now that these veterans have mostly retired or died, we are left in the hands of the generations which, having heard of microbes much as St Thomas Aquinas heard of angels, suddenly concluded that the whole art of healing could be summed up in the formula: Find the microbe and kill it. And even that they did not know how to do. The simplest way to kill most microbes is to throw them into an open street or river and let the sun shine on them, which explains the fact that when great cities have recklessly thrown all their sewage into the open river the water has sometimes been cleaner twenty miles below the city than thirty miles above it. But doctors instinctively avoid all facts that are reassuring, and eagerly swallow those that make it a marvel that anyone could possibly survive three days in an atmosphere consisting mainly of countless pathogenic germs. They conceive microbes as immortal until slain by a germicide administered by a duly qualified medical man. All through Europe people are adjured, by public notices and even under legal penalties, not to throw their microbes into the sunshine, but to collect them carefully in a handkerchief; shield the handkerchief from the sun in the darkness and warmth of the pocket; and send it to a laundry to be mixed up with everybody else's handkerchiefs, with results only too familiar to local health authorities.

In the first frenzy of microbe killing, surgical instruments were dipped in carbolic oil, which was a great improvement on not dipping them in anything at all and sim-

20

ply using them dirty; but as microbes are so fond of carbolic oil that they swarm in it, it was not a success from the anti-microbe point of view. Formalin was squirted into the circulation of consumptives until it was discovered that formalin nourishes the tubercle bacillus handsomely and kills men. The popular theory of disease is the common medical theory: namely, that every disease had its microbe duly created in the garden of Eden, and has been steadily propagating itself and producing widening circles of malignant disease ever since. It was plain from the first that if this had been even approximately true, the whole human race would have been wiped out by the plague long ago, and that every epidemic, instead of fading out as mysteriously as it rushed in, would spread over the whole world. It was also evident that the characteristic microbe of a disease might be a symptom instead of a cause. An unpunctual man is always in a hurry; but it does not follow that hurry is the cause of unpunctuality: on the contrary, what is the matter with the patient is sloth. When Florence Nightingale said bluntly that if you overcrowded your soldiers in dirty quarters there would be an outbreak of smallpox among them, she was snubbed as an ignorant female who did not know that smallpox can be produced only by the importation of its specific microbe.

If this was the line taken about smallpox, the microbe of which has never yet been run down and exposed under the microscope by the bacteriologist, what must have been the ardor of conviction as to tuberculosis, tetanus, enteric fever, Maltese fever, diphtheria, and the rest of the diseases in which the characteristic bacillus had been identified! When there was no bacillus it was assumed that, since no disease could exist without a bacillus, it was simply eluding observation. When the bacillus was found, as it frequently was, in persons who were not suffering from the disease, the theory was saved by simply calling the bacillus an impostor, or pseudo-bacillus. The same boundless credulity which the public exhibit as to a doctor's power of diagnosis was shewn by the doctors themselves as to the analytic microbe hunters. These witch finders would give you a certificate of the ultimate constitution of anything from a sample of the water from your well to a scrap of your lungs, for seven-and-sixpence. I do not suggest that the analysts were dishonest. No doubt they carried the analysis as far as they could afford to carry it for the money. No doubt also they could afford to carry it far enough to be of some use. But the fact remains that just as doctors perform for half-a-crown, without the least misgiving, operations which could not be thoroughly and safely performed with due scientific rigor and the requisite apparatus by an unaided private practitioner for less than some thousands of pounds, so did they proceed on the assumption that they could get the last word of science as to the constituents of their pathological samples for a two-hours cab fare.

ECONOMIC DIFFICULTIES OF IMMUNIZATION

I have heard doctors affirm and deny almost every possible proposition as to disease and treatment. I can remember the time when doctors no more dreamt of consumption and pneumonia being infectious than they now dream of sea-sickness being infectious, or than so great a clinical observer as Sydenham dreamt of smallpox being infectious. I have heard doctors deny that there is such a thing as infection. I have heard them deny the existence of hydrophobia as a specific disease differing from tetanus. I have heard them defend prophylactic measures and prophylactic legislation as the sole and certain salvation of mankind from zymotic disease; and I have heard them denounce both as malignant spreaders of cancer and lunacy. But the one objection I have never heard from a doctor is the objection that prophylaxis by the inoculatory methods most in vogue is an economic impossibility under our private practice system. They buy some stuff from somebody for a shilling, and inject a pennyworth of it under their patient's skin for half-a-crown, concluding that, since this primitive rite pays

22

the somebody and pays them, the problem of prophylaxis has been satisfactorily solved. The results are sometimes no worse than the ordinary results of dirt getting into cuts; but neither the doctor nor the patient is quite satisfied unless the inoculation "takes": that is, unless it produces perceptible illness and disablement. Sometimes both doctor and patient get more value in this direction than they bargain for. The results of ordinary private-practice-inoculation at their worst are bad enough to be indistinguishable from those of the most discreditable and dreaded disease known; and doctors, to save the credit of the inoculation, have been driven to accuse their patient or their patient's parents of having contracted this disease independently of the inoculation, an excuse which naturally does not make the family any more resigned, and leads to public recriminations in which the doctors, forgetting everything but the immediate quarrel, naively excuse themselves by admitting, and even claiming as a point in their favor, that it is often impossible to distinguish the disease produced by their inoculation and the disease they have accused the patient of contracting. And both parties assume that what is at issue is the scientific soundness of the prophylaxis. It never occurs to them that the particular pathogenic germ which they intended to introduce into the patient's system may be quite innocent of the catastrophe, and that the casual dirt introduced with it may be at fault. When, as in the case of smallpox or cowpox, the germ has not yet been detected, what you inoculate is simply undefined matter that has been scraped off an anything but chemically clean calf suffering from the disease in question. You take your chance of the germ being in the scrapings, and, lest you should kill it, you take no precautions against other germs being in it as well. Anything may happen as the result of such an inoculation. Yet this is the only stuff of the kind which is prepared and supplied even in State establishments: that is, in the only establishments free from the commercial temptation to adulterate materials and scamp precautionary processes.

23

PREFACE ON DOCTORS

Even if the germ were identified, complete precautions would hardly pay. It is true that microbe farming is not expensive. The cost of breeding and housing two head of cattle would provide for the breeding and housing of enough microbes to inoculate the entire population of the globe since human life first appeared on it. But the precautions necessary to insure that the inoculation shall consist of nothing else but the required germ in the proper state of attenuation are a very different matter from the precautions necessary in the distribution and consumption of beefsteaks. Yet people expect to find vaccines and anti-toxins and the like retailed at "popular prices" in private enterprise shops just as they expect to find ounces of tobacco and papers of pins.

THE PERILS OF INOCULATION

The trouble does not end with the matter to be inoculated. There is the question of the condition of the patient. The discoveries of Sir Almroth Wright have shewn that the appalling results which led to the hasty dropping in 1894 of Koch's tuberculin were not accidents, but perfectly orderly and inevitable phenomena following the injection of dangerously strong "vaccines" at the wrong moment, and reinforcing the disease instead of stimulating the resistance to it. To ascertain the right moment a laboratory and a staff of experts are needed. The general practitioner, having no such laboratory and no such experience, has always chanced it, and insisted, when he was unlucky, that the results were not due to the inoculation, but to some other cause: a favorite and not very tactful one being the drunkenness or licentiousness of the patient. But though a few doctors have now learnt the danger of inoculating without any reference to the patient's "opsonic index" at the moment of inoculation, and though those other doctors who are denouncing the danger as imaginary and opsonin as a craze or a fad, obviously do so because it involves an operation which they have neither the means nor the knowledge to perform, there is still no grasp of the economic change in the situa-

24

tion. They have never been warned that the practicability of any method of extirpating disease depends not only on its efficacy, but on its cost. For example, just at present the world has run raving mad on the subject of radium, which has excited our credulity precisely as the apparitions at Lourdes excited the credulity of Roman Catholics. Suppose it were ascertained that every child in the world could be rendered absolutely immune from all disease during its entire life by taking half an ounce of radium to every pint of its milk. The world would be none the healthier, because not even a Crown Prince—no, not even the son of a Chicago Meat King, could afford the treatment. Yet it is doubtful whether doctors would refrain from prescribing it on that ground. The recklessness with which they now recommend wintering in Egypt or at Davos to people who cannot afford to go to Cornwall, and the orders given for champagne jelly and old port in households where such luxuries must obviously be acquired at the cost of stinting necessaries, often make one wonder whether it is possible for a man to go through a medical training and retain a spark of common sense.

This sort of inconsiderateness gets cured only in the classes where poverty, pretentious as it is even at its worst, cannot pitch its pretences high enough to make it possible for the doctor (himself often no better off than the patient) to assume that the average income of an English family is about £2,000 a year, and that it is quite easy to break up a home, sell an old family seat at a sacrifice, and retire into a foreign sanatorium devoted to some "treatment" that did not exist two years ago and probably will not exist (except as a pretext for keeping an ordinary hotel) two years hence. In a poor practice the doctor must find cheap treatments for cheap people, or humiliate and lose his patients either by prescribing beyond their means or sending them to the public hospitals. When it comes to prophylactic inoculation, the alternative lies between the complete scientific process, which can only be brought down to a reasonable

25

PREFACE ON DOCTORS

cost by being very highly organized as a public service in a public institution, and such cheap, nasty, dangerous and scientifically spurious imitations as ordinary vaccination, which will probably be ended, like its equally vaunted forerunner, eighteenth century inoculation, by a purely reactionary law making all sorts of vaccination, scientific or not, criminal offences. Naturally, the poor doctor (that is, the average doctor) defends ordinary vaccination frantically, as it means to him the bread of his children. To secure the vehement and practically unanimous support of the rank and file of the medical profession for any sort of treatment or operation, all that is necessary is that it can be easily practised by a rather shabbily dressed man in a surgically dirty room in a surgically dirty house without any assistance, and that the materials for it shall cost, say, a penny, and the charge for it to a patient with £100 a year be half-a-crown. And, on the other hand, a hygienic measure has only to be one of such refinement, difficulty, precision and costliness as to be quite beyond the resources of private practice, to be ignored or angrily denounced as a fad.

TRADE UNIONISM AND SCIENCE

Here we have the explanation of the savage rancor that so amazes people who imagine that the controversy concerning vaccination is a scientific one. It has really nothing to do with science. The medical profession, consisting for the most part of very poor men struggling to keep up appearances beyond their means, find themselves threatened with the extinction of a considerable part of their incomes: a part, too, that is easily and regularly earned, since it is independent of disease, and brings every person born into the nation, healthy or not, to the doctors. To boot, there is the occasional windfall of an epidemic, with its panic and rush for revaccination. Under such circumstances, vaccination would be defended desperately were it twice as dirty, dangerous, and unscientific in method as it actually is. The note of fury in the defence, the feeling that the anti-vaccinator is doing a cruel, ruinous, inconsiderate thing in

26

a mood of malignant folly: all this, so puzzling to the observer who knows nothing of the economic side of the question, and only sees that the anti-vaccinator, having nothing whatever to gain and a good deal to lose by placing himself in opposition to the law and to the outcry that adds private persecution to legal penalties, can have no interest in the matter except the interest of a reformer in abolishing a corrupt and mischievous superstition, becomes intelligible the moment the tragedy of medical poverty and the lucrativeness of cheap vaccination is taken into account.

In the face of such economic pressure as this, it is silly to expect that medical teaching, any more than medical practice, can possibly be scientific. The test to which all methods of treatment are finally brought is whether they are lucrative to doctors or not. It would be difficult to cite any proposition less obnoxious to science than that advanced by Hahnemann: to wit, that drugs which in large doses produce certain symptoms, counteract them in very small doses, just as in more modern practice it is found that a sufficiently small inoculation with typhoid rallies our powers to resist the disease instead of prostrating us with it. But Hahnemann and his followers were frantically persecuted for a century by generations of apothecary-doctors whose incomes depended on the quantity of drugs they could induce their patients to swallow. These two cases of ordinary vaccination and homeopathy are typical of all the rest. Just as the object of a trade union under existing conditions must finally be, not to improve the technical quality of the work done by its members, but to secure a living wage for them, so the object of the medical profession today is to secure an income for the private doctor; and to this consideration all concern for science and public health must give way when the two come into conflict. Fortunately they are not always in conflict. Up to a certain point doctors, like carpenters and masons, must earn their living by doing the work that the public wants from them; and as it is not in the nature of things possible that such public want should be based on

PREFACE ON DOCTORS

unmixed disutility, it may be admitted that doctors have their uses, real as well as imaginary. But just as the best carpenter or mason will resist the introduction of a machine that is likely to throw him out of work, or the public technical education of unskilled laborers' sons to compete with him, so the doctor will resist with all his powers of persecution every advance of science that threatens his income. And as the advance of scientific hygiene tends to make the private doctor's visits rarer, and the public inspector's frequenter, whilst the advance of scientific therapeutics is in the direction of treatments that involve highly organized laboratories, hospitals, and public institutions generally, it unluckily happens that the organization of private practitioners which we call the medical profession is coming more and more to represent, not science, but desperate and embittered anti-science: a statement of things which is likely to get worse until the average doctor either depends upon or hopes for an appointment in the public health service for his livelihood.

So much for our guarantees as to medical science. Let us now deal with the more painful subject of medical kindness.

DOCTORS AND VIVISECTION

The importance to our doctors of a reputation for the tenderest humanity is so obvious, and the quantity of benevolent work actually done by them for nothing (a great deal of it from sheer good nature) so large, that at first sight it seems unaccountable that they should not only throw all their credit away, but deliberately choose to band themselves publicly with outlaws and scoundrels by claiming that in the pursuit of their professional knowledge they should be free from the restraints of law, of honor, of pity, of remorse, of everything that distinguishes an orderly citizen from a South Sea buccaneer, or a philosopher from an inquisitor. For here we look in vain for either an economic or a sentimental motive. In every generation fools and blackguards have made this claim; and honest and reasonable men, led by the strongest contemporary minds,

28

have repudiated it and exposed its crude rascality. From Shakespear and Dr Johnson to Ruskin and Mark Twain, the natural abhorrence of sane mankind for the vivisector's cruelty, and the contempt of able thinkers for his imbecile casuistry, have been expressed by the most popular spokesmen of humanity. If the medical profession were to outdo the Anti-Vivisection Societies in a general professional protest against the practice and principles of the vivisectors, every doctor in the kingdom would gain substantially by the immense relief and reconciliation which would follow such a reassurance of the humanity of the doctor. Not one doctor in a thousand is a vivisector, or has any interest in vivisection, either pecuniary or intellectual, or would treat his dog cruelly or allow anyone else to do it. It is true that the doctor complies with the professional fashion of defending vivisection, and assuring you that people like Shakespear and Dr Johnson and Ruskin and Mark Twain are ignorant sentimentalists, just as he complies with any other silly fashion: the mystery is, how it became the fashion in spite of its being so injurious to those who follow it. Making all possible allowance for the effect of the brazen lying of the few men who bring a rush of despairing patients to their doors by professing in letters to the newspapers to have learnt from vivisection how to cure certain diseases, and the assurances of the sayers of smooth things that the practice is quite painless under the law, it is still difficult to find any civilized motive for an attitude by which the medical profession has everything to lose and nothing to gain.

THE PRIMITIVE SAVAGE MOTIVE

I say civilized motive advisedly; for primitive tribal motives are easy enough to find. Every savage chief who is not a Mahomet learns that if he wishes to strike the imagination of his tribe—and without doing that he cannot rule them—he must terrify or revolt them from time to time by acts of hideous cruelty or disgusting unnaturalness. We are far from being as superior to such tribes as we imagine. It is very doubtful indeed whether Peter the Great could

29

have effected the changes he made in Russia if he had not fascinated and intimidated his people by his monstrous cruelties and grotesque escapades. Had he been a nineteenth-century king of England, he would have had to wait for some huge accidental calamity: a cholera epidemic, a war, or an insurrection, before waking us up sufficiently to get anything done. Vivisection helps the doctor to rule us as Peter ruled the Russians. The notion that the man who does dreadful things is superhuman, and that therefore he can also do wonderful things either as ruler, avenger, healer, or what not, is by no means confined to barbarians. Just as the manifold wickednesses and stupidities of our criminal code are supported, not by any general comprehension of law or study of jurisprudence, not even by simple vindictiveness, but by the superstition that a calamity of any sort must be expiated by a human sacrifice; so the wickednesses and stupidities of our medicine men are rooted in superstitions that have no more to do with science than the traditional ceremony of christening an ironclad has to do with the effectiveness of its armament. We have only to turn to Macaulay's description of the treatment of Charles II in his last illness to see how strongly his physicians felt that their only chance of cheating death was by outraging nature in tormenting and disgusting their unfortunate patient. True, this was more than two centuries ago; but I have heard my own nineteenth-century grandfather describe the cupping and firing and nauseous medicines of his time with perfect credulity as to their beneficial effects; and some more modern treatments appear to me quite as barbarous. It is in this way that vivisection pays the doctor. It appeals to the fear and credulity of the savage in us; and without fear and credulity half the private doctor's occupation and seven-eighths of his influence would be gone.

THE HIGHER MOTIVE. THE TREE OF KNOWLEDGE

But the greatest force of all on the side of vivisection is the mighty and indeed divine force of curiosity. Here we

have no decaying tribal instinct which men strive to root
out of themselves as they strive to root out the tiger's lust
for blood. On the contrary, the curiosity of the ape, or of
the child who pulls out the legs and wings of a fly to see
what it will do without them, or who, on being told that a
cat dropped out of the window will always fall on its legs,
immediately tries the experiment on the nearest cat from
the highest window in the house (I protest I did it myself
from the first floor only), is as nothing compared to the
thirst for knowledge of the philosopher, the poet, the biolo-
gist, and the naturalist. I have always despised Adam because he had to be tempted by the woman, as she was by
the serpent, before he could be induced to pluck the apple
from the tree of knowledge. I should have swallowed
every apple on the tree the moment the owner's back was
turned. When Gray said "Where ignorance is bliss, 'tis folly
to be wise," he forgot that it is godlike to be wise; and since
nobody wants bliss particularly, or could stand more than
a very brief taste of it if it were attainable, and since everybody, by the deepest law of the Life Force, desires to be
godlike, it is stupid, and indeed blasphemous and despairing, to hope that the thirst for knowledge will either dimin-
ish or consent to be subordinated to any other end whatso-
ever. We shall see later on that the claim that has arisen
in this way for the unconditioned pursuit of knowledge is
as idle as all dreams of unconditioned activity; but none
the less the right to knowledge must be regarded as a fundamental human right. The fact that men of science have had
to fight so hard to secure its recognition, and are still so
vigorously persecuted when they discover anything that is
not quite palatable to vulgar people, makes them sorely
jealous for that right; and when they hear a popular outcry
for the suppression of a method of research which has an
air of being scientific, their first instinct is to rally to the
defence of that method without further consideration, with
the result that they sometimes, as in the case of vivisection,
presently find themselves fighting on a false issue.

31

THE FLAW IN THE ARGUMENT

I may as well pause here to explain their error. The right to know is like the right to live. It is fundamental and unconditional in its assumption that knowledge, like life, is a desirable thing, though any fool can prove that ignorance is bliss, and that "a little knowledge is a dangerous thing" (a little being the most that any of us can attain), as easily as that the pains of life are more numerous and constant than its pleasures, and that therefore we should all be better dead. The logic is unimpeachable; but its only effect is to make us say that if these are the conclusions logic leads to, so much the worse for logic, after which curt dismissal of Folly, we continue living and learning by instinct: that is, as of right. We legislate on the assumption that no man may be killed on the strength of a demonstration that he would be happier in his grave, not even if he is dying slowly of cancer and begs the doctor to despatch him quickly and mercifully. To get killed lawfully he must violate somebody else's right to live by committing murder. But he is by no means free to live unconditionally. In society he can exercise his right to live only under very stiff conditions. In countries where there is compulsory military service he may even have to throw away his individual life to save the life of the community.

It is just so in the case of the right to knowledge. It is a right that is as yet very imperfectly recognized in practice. But in theory it is admitted that an adult person in pursuit of knowledge must not be refused it on the ground that he would be better or happier without it. Parents and priests may forbid knowledge to those who accept their authority; and social taboo may be made effective by acts of legal persecution under cover of repressing blasphemy, obscenity, and sedition; but no government now openly forbids its subjects to pursue knowledge on the ground that knowledge is in itself a bad thing, or that it is possible for any of us to have too much of it.

PREFACE ON DOCTORS
LIMITATIONS OF THE RIGHT TO KNOWLEDGE

But neither does any government exempt the pursuit of knowledge, any more than the pursuit of life, liberty, and happiness (as the American Constitution puts it), from all social conditions. No man is allowed to put his mother into the stove because he desires to know how long an adult woman will survive at a temperature of 500° Fahrenheit, no matter how important or interesting that particular addition to the store of human knowledge may be. A man who did so would have short work made not only of his right to knowledge, but of his right to live and all his other rights at the same time. The right to knowledge is not the only right; and its exercise must be limited by respect for other rights, and for its own exercise by others. When a man says to Society, "May I torture my mother in pursuit of knowledge?" Society replies "No." If he pleads, "What! Not even if I have a chance of finding out how to cure cancer by doing it?" Society still says, "Not even then." If the scientist, making the best of his disappointment, goes on to ask may he torture a dog, the stupid and callous people who do not realize that a dog is a fellow-creature, and sometimes a good friend, may say Yes, though Shakespear, Dr Johnson and their like may say No. But even those who say "You may torture *a* dog" never say "You may torture *my* dog." And nobody says, "Yes, because in the pursuit of knowledge you may do as you please." Just as even the stupidest people say, in effect, "If you cannot attain to knowledge without burning your mother you must do without knowledge," so the wisest people say, "If you cannot attain to knowledge without torturing a dog, you must do without knowledge."

A FALSE ALTERNATIVE

But in practice you cannot persuade any wise man that this alternative can ever be forced on anyone but a fool, or that a fool can be trusted to learn anything from any ex-

PREFACE ON DOCTORS

periment, cruel or humane. The Chinaman who burnt down his house to roast his pig was no doubt honestly unable to conceive any less disastrous way of cooking his dinner; and the roast must have been spoiled after all (a perfect type of the average vivisectionist experiment); but this did not prove that the Chinaman was right: it only proved that the Chinaman was an incapable cook and, fundamentally, a fool.

Take another celebrated experiment: one in sanitary reform. In the days of Nero Rome was in the same predicament as London today. If someone would burn down London, and it were rebuilt, as it would now have to be, subject to the sanitary by-laws and Building Act provisions enforced by the London County Council, it would be enormously improved; and the average lifetime of Londoners would be considerably prolonged. Nero argued in the same way about Rome. He employed incendiaries to set it on fire; and he played the harp in scientific raptures whilst it was burning. I am so far of Nero's way of thinking that I have often said, when consulted by despairing sanitary reformers, that what London needs to make her healthy is an earthquake. Why, then, it may be asked, do not I, as a public-spirited man, employ incendiaries to set it on fire, with a heroic disregard of the consequences to myself and others? Any vivisector would, if he had the courage of his opinions. The reasonable answer is that London can be made healthy without burning her down; and that as we have not enough civic virtue to make her healthy in a humane and economical way, we should not have enough to rebuild her in that way. In the old Hebrew legend, God lost patience with the world as Nero did with Rome, and drowned everybody except a single family. But the result was that the progeny of that family reproduced all the vices of their predecessors so exactly that the misery caused by the flood might just as well have been spared: things went on just as they did before. In the same way, the list of

34

PREFACE ON DOCTORS

diseases which vivisection claims to have cured is long; but the returns of the Registrar-General shew that people still persist in dying of them as if vivisection had never been heard of. Any fool can burn down a city or cut an animal open; and an exceptionally foolish fool is quite likely to promise enormous benefits to the race as the result of such activities. But when the constructive, benevolent part of the business comes to be done, the same want of imagination, the same stupidity and cruelty, the same laziness and want of perseverance that prevented Nero or the vivisector from devising or pushing through humane methods, prevents him from bringing order out of the chaos and happiness out of the misery he has made. At one time it seemed reasonable enough to declare that it was impossible to find whether or not there was a stone inside a man's body except by exploring it with a knife, or to find out what the sun is made of without visiting it in a balloon. Both these impossibilities have been achieved, but not by vivisectors. The Röntgen rays need not hurt the patient; and spectrum analysis involves no destruction. After such triumphs of humane experiment and reasoning, it is useless to assure us that there is no other key to knowledge except cruelty. When the vivisector offers us that assurance, we reply simply and contemptuously, "You mean that you are not clever or humane or energetic enough to find one."

CRUELTY FOR ITS OWN SAKE

It will now, I hope, be clear why the attack on vivisection is not an attack on the right to knowledge: why, indeed, those who have the deepest conviction of the sacredness of that right are the leaders of the attack. No knowledge is finally impossible of human attainment; for even though it may be beyond our present capacity, the needed capacity is not unattainable. Consequently no method of investigation is the only method; and no law forbidding any particular method can cut us off from the knowledge we hope to gain by it. The only knowledge we lose by for-

PREFACE ON DOCTORS

bidding cruelty is knowledge at first hand of cruelty itself, which is precisely the knowledge humane people wish to be spared.

But the question remains: Do we all really wish to be spared that knowledge? Are humane methods really to be preferred to cruel ones? Even if the experiments come to nothing, may not their cruelty be enjoyed for its own sake, as a sensational luxury? Let us face these questions boldly, not shrinking from the fact that cruelty is one of the primitive pleasures of mankind, and that the detection of its Protean disguises as law, education, medicine, discipline, sport and so forth, is one of the most difficult of the unending tasks of the legislator.

OUR OWN CRUELTIES

At first blush it may seem not only unnecessary, but even indecent, to discuss such a proposition as the elevation of cruelty to the rank of a human right. Unnecessary, because no vivisector confesses to a love of cruelty for its own sake or claims any general fundamental right to be cruel. Indecent, because there is an accepted convention to repudiate cruelty; and vivisection is only tolerated by the law on condition that, like judicial torture, it shall be done as mercifully as the nature of the practice allows. But the moment the controversy becomes embittered, the recriminations bandied between the opposed parties bring us face-to-face with some very ugly truths. On one occasion I was invited to speak at a large Anti-Vivisection meeting in the Queen's Hall in London. I found myself on the platform with fox hunters, tame stag hunters, men and women whose calendar was divided, not by pay days and quarter days, but by seasons for killing animals for sport: the fox, the hare, the otter, the partridge and the rest having each its appointed date for slaughter. The ladies among us wore hats and cloaks and head-dresses obtained by wholesale massacres, ruthless trappings, callous extermination of our fellow creatures. We insisted on our butchers supplying us with white veal, and were large and constant consumers of *pâté*

36

de foie gras: both comestibles being obtained by revolting methods. We sent our sons to public schools where indecent flogging is a recognized method of taming the young human animal. Yet we were all in hysterics of indignation at the cruelties of the vivisectors. These, if any were present, must have smiled sardonically at such inhuman humanitarians, whose daily habits and fashionable amusements cause more suffering in England in a week than all the vivisectors of Europe do in a year. I made a very effective speech, not exclusively against vivisection, but against cruelty; and I have never been asked to speak since by that Society, nor do I expect to be, as I should probably give such offence to its most affluent subscribers that its attempts to suppress vivisection would be seriously hindered. But that does not prevent the vivisectors from freely using the "youre another" retort, and using it with justice.

We must therefore give ourselves no airs of superiority when denouncing the cruelties of vivisection. We all do just as horrible things, with even less excuse. But in making that admission we are also making short work of the virtuous airs with which we are sometimes referred to the humanity of the medical profession as a guarantee that vivisection is not abused—much as if our burglars should assure us that they are too honest to abuse the practice of burglaring. We are, as a matter of fact, a cruel nation; and our habit of disguising our vices by giving polite names to the offences we are determined to commit, does not, unfortunately for my own comfort, impose on me. Vivisectors can hardly pretend to be better than the classes from which they are drawn, or those above them; and if these classes are capable of sacrificing animals in various cruel ways under cover of sport, fashion, education, discipline, and even, when the cruel sacrifices are human sacrifices, of political economy, it is idle for the vivisector to pretend that he is incapable of practising cruelty for pleasure or profit or both under the cloak of science. We are all tarred with the same brush; and the vivisectors are not slow to remind us of it, and to protest

37

vehemently against being branded as exceptionally cruel and as devisers of horrible instruments of torture by people whose main notion of enjoyment is cruel sport, and whose requirements in the way of villainously cruel traps occupy pages of the catalogue of the Army and Navy Stores.

THE SCIENTIFIC INVESTIGATION OF CRUELTY

There is in man a specific lust for cruelty which infects even his passion of pity and makes it savage. Simple disgust at cruelty is very rare. The people who turn sick and faint and those who gloat are often alike in the pains they take to witness executions, floggings, operations or any other exhibitions of suffering, especially those involving bloodshed, blows, and laceration. A craze for cruelty can be developed just as a craze for drink can; and nobody who attempts to ignore cruelty as a possible factor in the attraction of vivisection and even of anti-vivisection, or in the credulity with which we accept its excuses, can be regarded as a scientific investigator of it. Those who accuse vivisectors of indulging the well-known passion of cruelty under the cloak of research are therefore putting forward a strictly scientific psychological hypothesis, which is also simple, human, obvious, and probable. It may be as wounding to the personal vanity of the vivisector as Darwin's Origin of Species was to the people who could not bear to think that they were cousins to the monkeys (remember Goldsmith's anger when he was told that he could not move his upper jaw); but science has to consider only the truth of the hypothesis, and not whether conceited people will like it or not. In vain do the sentimental champions of vivisection declare themselves the most humane of men, inflicting suffering only to relieve it, scrupulous in the use of anesthetics, and void of all passion except the passion of pity for a disease-ridden world. The really scientific investigator answers that the question cannot be settled by hysterical protestations, and that if the vivisectionist rejects deductive

38

reasoning, he had better clear his character by his own favorite method of experiment.

SUGGESTED LABORATORY TESTS OF THE VIVISECTOR'S EMOTIONS

Take the hackneyed case of the Italian who tortured mice, ostensibly to find out about the effects of pain rather less than the nearest dentist could have told him, and who boasted of the ecstatic sensations (he actually used the word love) with which he carried out his experiments. Or the gentleman who starved sixty dogs to death to establish the fact that a dog deprived of food gets progressively lighter and weaker, becoming remarkably emaciated, and finally dying: an undoubted truth, but ascertainable without laboratory experiments by a simple enquiry addressed to the nearest policeman, or, failing him, to any sane person in Europe. The Italian is diagnosed as a cruel voluptuary: the dog-starver is passed over as such a hopeless fool that it is impossible to take any interest in him. Why not test the diagnosis scientifically? Why not perform a careful series of experiments on persons under the influence of voluptuous ecstasy, so as to ascertain its physiological symptoms? Then perform a second series on persons engaged in mathematical work or machine designing, so as to ascertain the symptoms of cold scientific activity? Then note the symptoms of a vivisector performing a cruel experiment; and compare them with the voluptuary symptoms and the mathematical symptoms? Such experiments would be quite as interesting and important as any yet undertaken by the vivisectors. They might open a line of investigation which would finally make, for instance, the ascertainment of the guilt or innocence of an accused person a much exacter process than the very fallible methods of our criminal courts. But instead of proposing such an investigation, our vivisectors offer us all the pious protestations and all the huffy recriminations that any common unscientific mortal offers when he is accused of unworthy conduct.

39

ROUTINE

Yet most vivisectors would probably come triumphant out of such a series of experiments, because vivisection is now a routine, like butchering or hanging or flogging; and many of the men who practise it do so only because it has been established as part of the profession they have adopted. Far from enjoying it, they have simply overcome their natural repugnance and become indifferent to it, as men inevitably become indifferent to anything they do often enough. It is this dangerous power of custom that makes it so difficult to convince the common sense of mankind that any established commercial or professional practice has its root in passion. Let a routine once spring from passion, and you will presently find thousands of routineers following it passionlessly for a livelihood. Thus it always seems strained to speak of the religious convictions of a clergyman, because nine out of ten clergymen have no religious convictions: they are ordinary officials carrying on a routine of baptizing, marrying, and churching; praying, reciting, and preaching; and, like solicitors or doctors, getting away from their duties with relief to hunt, to garden, to keep bees, to go into society, and the like. In the same way many people do cruel and vile things without being in the least cruel or vile, because the routine to which they have been brought up is superstitiously cruel and vile. To say that every man who beats his children and every schoolmaster who flogs a pupil is a conscious debauchee is absurd: thousands of dull, conscientious people beat their children conscientiously, because they were beaten themselves and think children ought to be beaten. The ill-tempered vulgarity that instinctively strikes at and hurts a thing that annoys it (and all children are annoying), and the simple stupidity that requires from a child perfection beyond the reach of the wisest and best adults (perfect truthfulness coupled with perfect obedience is quite a common condition of leaving a child unwhipped), produce a good deal of flagellation among people who not only do not lust after it, but who hit the harder because they

40

are angry at having to perform an uncomfortable duty. These people will beat merely to assert their authority, or to carry out what they conceive to be a divine order on the strength of the precept of Solomon recorded in the Bible, which carefully adds that Solomon completely spoiled his own son and turned away from the god of his fathers to the sensuous idolatry in which he ended his days.

In the same way we find men and women practising vivisection as senselessly as a humane butcher, who adores his fox terrier, will cut a calf's throat and hang it up by its heels to bleed slowly to death because it is the custom to eat veal and insist on its being white; or as a German purveyor nails a goose to a board and stuffs it with food because fashionable people eat *pâté de foie gras;* or as the crew of a whaler breaks in on a colony of seals and clubs them to death in wholesale massacre because ladies want sealskin jackets; or as fanciers blind singing birds with hot needles, and mutilate the ears and tails of dogs and horses. Let cruelty or kindness or anything else once become customary and it will be practised by people to whom it is not at all natural, but whose rule of life is simply to do only what everybody else does, and who would lose their employment and starve if they indulged in any peculiarity. A respectable man will lie daily, in speech and in print, about the qualities of the article he lives by selling, because it is customary to do so. He will flog his boy for telling a lie, because it is customary to do so. He will also flog him for not telling a lie if the boy tells inconvenient or disrespectful truths, because it is customary to do so. He will give the same boy a present on his birthday, and buy him a spade and bucket at the seaside, because it is customary to do so, being all the time neither particularly mendacious, nor particularly cruel, nor particularly generous, but simply incapable of ethical judgment or independent action.

Just so do we find a crowd of petty vivisectionists daily committing atrocities and stupidities, because it is the custom to do so. Vivisection is customary as part of the routine of

41

preparing lectures in medical schools. For instance, there are two ways of making the action of the heart visible to students. One, a barbarous, ignorant, and thoughtless way, is to stick little flags into a rabbit's heart and let the students see the flags jump. The other, an elegant, ingenious, well-informed, and instructive way, is to put a sphygmograph on the student's wrist and let him see a record of his heart's action traced by a needle on a slip of smoked paper. But it has become the custom for lecturers to teach from the rabbit; and the lecturers are not original enough to get out of their groove. Then there are the demonstrations which are made by cutting up frogs with scissors. The most humane man, however repugnant the operation may be to him at first, cannot do it at lecture after lecture for months without finally—and that very soon—feeling no more for the frog than if he were cutting up pieces of paper. Such clumsy and lazy ways of teaching are based on the cheapness of frogs and rabbits. If machines were as cheap as frogs, engineers would not only be taught the anatomy of machines and the functions of their parts: they would also have machines misused and wrecked before them so that they might learn as much as possible by using their eyes, and as little as possible by using their brains and imaginations. Thus we have, as part of the routine of teaching, a routine of vivisection which soon produces complete indifference to it on the part even of those who are naturally humane. If they pass on from the routine of lecture preparation, not into general practice, but into research work, they carry this acquired indifference with them into the laboratory, where any atrocity is possible, because all atrocities satisfy curiosity. The routine man is in the majority in his profession always: consequently the moment his practice is tracked down to its source in human passion there is a great and quite sincere poohpoohing from himself, from the mass of the profession, and from the mass of the public, which sees that the average doctor is much too commonplace and

PREFACE ON DOCTORS
decent a person to be capable of passionate wickedness of
any kind.

Here, then, we have in vivisection, as in all the other
tolerated and instituted cruelties, this anti-climax: that
only a negligible percentage of those who practise and consequently defend it get any satisfaction out of it. As in Mr
Galsworthy's play Justice the useless and detestable torture of solitary imprisonment is shewn at its worst without
the introduction of a single cruel person into the drama, so
it would be possible to represent all the torments of vivisection dramatically without introducing a single vivisector
who had not felt sick at his first experience in the laboratory.
Not that this can exonerate any vivisector from suspicion of
enjoying his work (or *her* work: a good deal of the vivisection in medical schools is done by women). In every
autobiography which records a real experience of school
or prison life, we find that here and there among the routineers there is to be found the genuine amateur, the orgi-
astic flogging schoolmaster or the nagging warder, who has
sought out a cruel profession for the sake of its cruelty. But
it is the genuine routineer who is the bulwark of the practice, because, though you can excite public fury against a
Sade, a Bluebeard, or a Nero, you cannot rouse any feeling
against dull Mr Smith doing his duty: that is, doing the
usual thing. He is so obviously no better and no worse than
anyone else that it is difficult to conceive that the things
he does are abominable. If you would see public dislike
surging up in a moment against an individual, you must
watch one who does something unusual, no matter how
sensible it may be. The name of Jonas Hanway lives as that
of a brave man because he was the first who dared to appear in the streets of this rainy island with an umbrella.

THE OLD LINE BETWEEN MAN AND
BEAST

But there is still a distinction to be clung to by those
who dare not tell themselves the truth about the medical

43

profession because they are so helplessly dependent on it
when death threatens the household. That distinction is the
line that separates the brute from the man in the old clas-
sification. Granted, they will plead, that we are all cruel;
yet the tame stag hunter does not hunt men; and the
sportsman who lets a leash of greyhounds loose on a hare
would be horrified at the thought of letting them loose on
a human child. The lady who gets her cloak by flaying a
sable does not flay a negro; nor does it ever occur to her
that her veal cutlet might be improved on by a slice of
tender baby.

Now there was a time when some trust could be placed
in this distinction. The Roman Catholic Church still main-
tains, with what it must permit me to call a stupid obstinacy,
and in spite of St Francis and St Anthony, that animals
have no souls and no rights; so that you cannot sin against
an animal, or against God by anything you may choose to
do to an animal. Resisting the temptation to enter on an
argument as to whether you may not sin against your own
soul if you are unjust or cruel to the least of those whom
St Francis called his little brothers, I have only to point
out here that nothing could be more despicably superstitious
in the opinion of a vivisector than the notion that science
recognizes any such step in evolution as the step from a
physical organism to an immortal soul. That conceit has
been taken out of all our men of science, and out of all our
doctors, by the evolutionists; and when it is considered how
completely obsessed biological science has become in our
days, not by the full scope of evolution, but by that particular method of it which has neither sense nor purpose nor
life nor anything human, much less godlike, in it: by the
method, that is, of so-called Natural Selection (meaning
no selection at all, but mere dead accident and luck), the
folly of trusting to vivisectors to hold the human animal
any more sacred than the other animals becomes so clear
that it would be waste of time to insist further on it. As a
matter of fact the man who once concedes to the vivisector

44

the right to put a dog outside the laws of honor and fellowship, concedes to him also the right to put himself outside them; for he is nothing to the vivisector but a more highly developed, and consequently more interesting-to-experiment-on vertebrate than the dog.

VIVISECTING THE HUMAN SUBJECT

I have in my hand a printed and published account by a doctor of how he tested his remedy for pulmonary tuberculosis, which was, to inject a powerful germicide directly into the circulation by stabbing a vein with a syringe. He was one of those doctors who are able to command public sympathy by saying, quite truly, that when they discovered that the proposed treatment was dangerous, they experimented thenceforth on themselves. In this case the doctor was devoted enough to carry his experiments to the point of running serious risks, and actually making himself very uncomfortable. But he did not begin with himself. His first experiment was on two hospital patients. On receiving a message from the hospital to the effect that these two martyrs to therapeutic science had all but expired of convulsions, he experimented on a rabbit, which instantly dropped dead. It was then, and not until then, that he began to experiment on himself, with the germicide modified in the direction indicated by the experiments made on the two patients and the rabbit. As a good many people countenance vivisection because they fear that if the experiments are not made on rabbits they will be made on themselves, it is worth noting that in this case, where both rabbits and men were equally available, the men, being of course enormously more instructive and costing nothing, were experimented on first. Once grant the ethics of the vivisectionists and you not only sanction the experiment on the human subject, but make it the first duty of the vivisector. If a guinea pig may be sacrificed for the sake of the very little that can be learnt from it, shall not a man be sacrificed for the sake of the great deal that can be learnt from him? At all events, he *is* sacrificed, as this typical case shows. I may add (not that

45

it touches the argument) that the doctor, the patients, and the rabbit all suffered in vain, as far as the hoped-for rescue of the race from pulmonary consumption is concerned.

"THE LIE IS A EUROPEAN POWER"

Now at the very time when the lectures describing these experiments were being circulated in print and discussed eagerly by the medical profession, the customary denials that patients are experimented on were as loud, as indignant, as high-minded as ever, in spite of the few intelligent doctors who point out rightly that all treatments are experiments on the patient. And this brings us to an obvious but mostly overlooked weakness in the vivisector's position: that is, his inevitable forfeiture of all claim to have his word believed. It is hardly to be expected that a man who does not hesitate to vivisect for the sake of science will hesitate to lie about it afterwards to protect it from what he deems the ignorant sentimentality of the laity. When the public conscience stirs uneasily and threatens suppression, there is never wanting some doctor of eminent position and high character who will sacrifice himself devotedly to the cause of science by coming forward to assure the public on his honor that all experiments on animals are completely painless; although he must know that the very experiments which first provoked the anti-vivisection movement by their atrocity were experiments to ascertain the physiological effects of the sensation of extreme pain (the much more interesting physiology of pleasure remains uninvestigated) and that all experiments in which sensation is a factor are voided by its suppression. Besides, vivisection may be painless in cases where the experiments are very cruel. If a person scratches me with a poisoned dagger so gently that I do not feel the scratch, he has achieved a painless vivisection; but if I presently die in torment I am not likely to consider that his humanity is amply vindicated by his gentleness. A cobra's bite hurts so little that the creature is almost, legally speaking, a vivisector who inflicts no pain. By giving his victims chloroform before biting them he could comply with

46

the law completely.

Here, then, is a pretty deadlock. Public support of vivisection is founded almost wholly on the assurances of the vivisectors that great public benefits may be expected from the practice. Not for a moment do I suggest that such a defence would be valid even if proved. But when the witnesses begin by alleging that in the cause of science all the customary ethical obligations (which include the obligation to tell the truth) are suspended, what weight can any reasonable person give to their testimony? I would rather swear fifty lies than take an animal which had licked my hand in good fellowship and torture it. If I did torture the dog, I should certainly not have the face to turn round and ask how any person dare suspect an honorable man like myself of telling lies. Most sensible and humane people would, I hope, reply flatly that honorable men do not behave dishonorably even to dogs. The murderer who, when asked by the chaplain whether he had any other crimes to confess, replied indignantly "What do you take me for?" reminds us very strongly of the vivisectors who are so deeply hurt when their evidence is set aside as worthless.

AN ARGUMENT WHICH WOULD DEFEND ANY CRIME

The Achilles heel of vivisection, however, is not to be found in the pain it causes, but in the line of argument by which it is justified. The medical code regarding it is simply criminal anarchism at its very worst. Indeed, no criminal has yet had the impudence to argue as every vivisector argues. No burglar contends that as it is admittedly important to have money to spend, and as the object of burglary is to provide the burglar with money to spend, and as in many instances it has achieved this object, therefore the burglar is a public benefactor and the police are ignorant sentimentalists. No highway robber has yet harrowed us with denunciations of the puling moralist who allows his child to suffer all the evils of poverty because certain faddists think it dishonest to garotte an alderman. Thieves and

47

assassins understand quite well that there are paths of acquisition, even of the best things, that are barred to all men
of honor. Again, has the silliest burglar ever pretended that
to put a stop to burglary is to put a stop to industry? All
the vivisections that have been performed since the world
began have produced nothing so important as the innocent
and honorable discovery of radiography; and one of the
reasons why radiography was not discovered sooner was
that the men whose business it was to discover new clinical
methods were coarsening and stupefying themselves with
the sensual villanies and cutthroat's casuistries of vivisection. The law of the conservation of energy holds good in
physiology as in other things: every vivisector is a deserter
from the army of honorable investigators. But the vivisector
does not see this. He not only calls his methods scientific:
he contends that there are no other scientific methods. When
you express your natural loathing for his cruelty and your
natural contempt for his stupidity, he imagines that you are
attacking science. Yet he has no inkling of the method and
temper of science. The point at issue being plainly whether
he is a rascal or not, he not only insists that the real point
is whether some hot-headed anti-vivisectionist is a liar
(which he proves by ridiculously unscientific assumptions
as to the degree of accuracy attainable in human statement),
but never dreams of offering any scientific evidence by his
own methods.

There are many paths to knowledge already discovered; and no enlightened man doubts that there are many
more waiting to be discovered. Indeed, all paths lead to
knowledge; because even the vilest and stupidest action
teaches us something about vileness and stupidity, and may
accidentally teach us a good deal more: for instance, a cutthroat learns (and perhaps teaches) the anatomy of the
carotid artery and jugular vein; and there can be no question that the burning of St Joan of Arc must have been a
most instructive and interesting experiment to a good observer, and could have been made more so if it had been

48

carried out by skilled physiologists under laboratory conditions. The earthquake in San Francisco proved invaluable as an experiment in the stability of giant steel buildings; and the ramming of the Victoria by the Camperdown settled doubtful points of the greatest importance in naval warfare. According to vivisectionist logic our builders would be justified in producing artificial earthquakes with dynamite, and our admirals in contriving catastrophes at naval manœuvres, in order to follow up the line of research thus accidentally discovered.

The truth is, if the acquisition of knowledge justifies every sort of conduct, it justifies any sort of conduct, from the illumination of Nero's feasts by burning human beings alive (another interesting experiment) to the simplest act of kindness. And in the light of that truth it is clear that the exemption of the pursuit of knowledge from the laws of honor is the most hideous conceivable enlargement of anarchy; worse, by far, than an exemption of the pursuit of money or political power, since these can hardly be attained without some regard for at least the appearances of human welfare, whereas a curious devil might destroy the whole race in torment, acquiring knowledge all the time from his highly interesting experiment. There is more danger in one respectable scientist countenancing such a monstrous claim than in fifty assassins or dynamitards. The man who makes it is ethically imbecile; and whoever imagines that it is a scientific claim has not the faintest conception of what science means. The paths to knowledge are countless. One of these paths is a path through darkness, secrecy, and cruelty. When a man deliberately turns from all other paths and goes down that one, it is scientific to infer that what attracts him is not knowledge, since there are other paths to that, but cruelty. With so strong and scientific a case against him, it is childish for him to stand on his honor and reputation and high character and the credit of a noble profession and so forth: he must clear himself either by reason or by experiment, unless he boldly contends that

49

evolution has retained a passion of cruelty in man just because it is indispensable to the fulness of his knowledge.

THOU ART THE MAN

I shall not be at all surprised if what I have written above has induced in sympathetic readers a transport of virtuous indignation at the expense of the medical profession. I shall not damp so creditable and salutary a sentiment; but I must point out that the guilt is shared by all of us. It is not in his capacity of healer and man of science that the doctor vivisects or defends vivisection, but in his entirely vulgar lay capacity. He is made of the same clay as the ignorant, shallow, credulous, half-miseducated, pecuniarily anxious people who call him in when they have tried in vain every bottle and every pill the advertizing druggist can persuade them to buy. The real remedy for vivisection is the remedy for all the mischief that the medical profession and all the other professions are doing: namely, more knowledge. The juries which send the poor Peculiars to prison, and give vivisectionists heavy damages against humane persons who accuse them of cruelty; the editors and councillors and student-led mobs who are striving to make Vivisection one of the watchwords of our civilization, are not doctors: they are the British public, all so afraid to die that they will cling frantically to any idol which promises to cure all their diseases, and crucify anyone who tells them that they must not only die when their time comes, but die like gentlemen. In their paroxysms of cowardice and selfishness they force the doctors to humor their folly and ignorance. How complete and inconsiderate their ignorance is can only be realized by those who have some knowledge of vital statistics, and of the illusions which beset Public Health legislation.

WHAT THE PUBLIC WANTS AND WILL NOT GET

The demands of this poor public are not reasonable, but they are quite simple. It dreads disease and desires to be protected against it. But it is poor and wants to be protected cheaply. Scientific measures are too hard to understand, too costly, too clearly tending towards a rise in the rates and more public interference with the insanitary, because insufficiently financed, private house. What the public wants, therefore, is a cheap magic charm to prevent, and a cheap pill or potion to cure all disease. It forces all such charms on the doctors.

THE VACCINATION CRAZE

Thus it was really the public and not the medical profession that took up vaccination with irresistible faith, sweeping the invention out of Jenner's hands and establishing it in a form which he himself repudiated. Jenner was not a man of science; but he was not a fool; and when he found that people who had suffered from cowpox either by contagion in the milking shed or by vaccination, were not, as he had supposed, immune from smallpox, he ascribed the cases of immunity which had formerly misled him to a disease of the horse, which, perhaps because we do not drink its milk and eat its flesh, is kept at a greater distance in our imagination than our foster mother the cow. At all events, the public, which had been boundlessly credulous about the cow, would not have the horse on any terms; and to this day the law which prescribes Jennerian vaccination is carried out with an anti-Jennerian inoculation because the public would have it so in spite of Jenner. All the grossest lies and superstitions which have disgraced the vaccination craze were taught to the doctors by the public. It was not the doctors who first began to declare that all our old men remember the time when almost every face they saw in the street was horribly pitted with smallpox, and that all this disfigurement has vanished since the introduction of vaccination. Jenner himself alluded to this imaginary phenomenon before the introduction of vaccination, and attributed it to the older practice of smallpox inoculation, by which Voltaire, Catherine II and Lady Mary Wortley Montagu so confidently expected to see the disease made harmless. It was not Jenner who set people declaring that smallpox,

51

PREFACE ON DOCTORS

if not abolished by vaccination, had at least been made much milder: on the contrary, he recorded a pre-vaccination epidemic in which none of the persons attacked went to bed or considered themselves as seriously ill. Neither Jenner, nor any other doctor ever, as far as I know, inculcated the popular notion that everybody got smallpox as a matter of course before vaccination was invented. That doctors get infected with these delusions, and are in their unprofessional capacity as members of the public subject to them like other men, is true; but if we had to decide whether vaccination was first forced on the public by the doctors or on the doctors by the public, we should have to decide against the public.

STATISTICAL ILLUSIONS

Public ignorance of the laws of evidence and of statistics can hardly be exaggerated. There may be a doctor here and there who in dealing with the statistics of disease has taken at least the first step towards sanity by grasping the fact that as an attack of even the commonest disease is an exceptional event, apparently overwhelming statistical evidence in favor of any prophylactic can be produced by persuading the public that everybody caught the disease formerly. Thus if a disease is one which normally attacks fifteen per cent of the population, and if the effect of a prophylactic is actually to increase the proportion to twenty per cent, the publication of this figure of twenty per cent will convince the public that the prophylactic has reduced the percentage by eighty per cent instead of increasing it by five, because the public, left to itself and to the old gentlemen who are always ready to remember, on every possible subject, that things used to be much worse than they are now (such old gentlemen greatly outnumber the laudatores tempori acti), will assume that the former percentage was about 100. The vogue of the Pasteur treatment of hydrophobia, for instance, was due to the assumption by the public that every person bitten by a rabid dog necessarily got hydrophobia. I myself heard hydrophobia discussed in my youth by doctors in Dublin before a Pasteur Institute ex-

52

isted, the subject having been brought forward there by the scepticism of an eminent surgeon as to whether hydrophobia is really a specific disease or only ordinary tetanus induced (as tetanus was then supposed to be induced) by a lacerated wound. There were no statistics available as to the proportion of dog bites that ended in hydrophobia; but nobody ever guessed that the cases could be more than two or three per cent of the bites. On me, therefore, the results published by the Pasteur Institute produced no such effect as they did on the ordinary man who thinks that the bite of a mad dog means certain hydrophobia. It seemed to me that the proportion of deaths among the cases treated at the Institute was rather higher, if anything, than might have been expected had there been no Institute in existence. But to the public every Pasteur patient who did not die was miraculously saved from an agonizing death by the beneficent white magic of that most trusty of all wizards, the man of science.

Even trained statisticians often fail to appreciate the extent to which statistics are vitiated by the unrecorded assumptions of their interpreters. Their attention is too much occupied with the cruder tricks of those who make a corrupt use of statistics for advertizing purposes. There is, for example, the percentage dodge. In some hamlet, barely large enough to have a name, two people are attacked during a smallpox epidemic. One dies: the other recovers. One has vaccination marks: the other has none. Immediately either the vaccinists or the anti-vaccinists publish the triumphant news that at such and such a place not a single vaccinated person died of smallpox whilst 100 per cent of the unvaccinated perished miserably; or, as the case may be, that 100 per cent of the unvaccinated recovered whilst the vaccinated succumbed to the last man. Or, to take another common instance, comparisons which are really comparisons between two social classes with different standards of nutrition and education are palmed off as comparisons between the results of a certain medical treatment and its neglect. Thus

53

it is easy to prove that the wearing of tall hats and the carrying of umbrellas enlarges the chest, prolongs life, and confers comparative immunity from disease; for the statistics shew that the classes which use these articles are bigger, healthier, and live longer than the class which never dreams of possessing such things. It does not take much perspicacity to see that what really makes this difference is not the tall hat and the umbrella, but the wealth and nourishment of which they are evidence, and that a gold watch or membership of a club in Pall Mall might be proved in the same way to have the like sovereign virtues. A university degree, a daily bath, the owning of thirty pairs of trousers, a knowledge of Wagner's music, a pew in church, anything, in short, that implies more means and better nurture than the mass of laborers enjoy, can be statistically palmed off as a magic-spell conferring all sorts of privileges.

In the case of a prophylactic enforced by law, this illusion is intensified grotesquely, because only vagrants can evade it. Now vagrants have little power of resisting any disease: their death-rate and their case-mortality rate is always high relatively to that of respectable folk. Nothing is easier, therefore, than to prove that compliance with any public regulation produces the most gratifying results. It would be equally easy even if the regulation actually raised the death-rate, provided it did not raise it sufficiently to make the average householder, who cannot evade regulations, die as early as the average vagrant who can.

THE SURPRISES OF ATTENTION AND NEGLECT

There is another statistical illusion which is independent of class differences. A common complaint of houseowners is that the Public Health Authorities frequently compel them to instal costly sanitary appliances which are condemned a few years later as dangerous to health, and forbidden under penalties. Yet these discarded mistakes are always made in the first instance on the strength of a demonstration that their introduction has reduced the death-rate. The explana-

54

tion is simple. Suppose a law were made that every child in the nation should be compelled to drink a pint of brandy per month, but that the brandy must be administered only when the child was in good health, with its digestion and so forth working normally, and its teeth either naturally or artificially sound. Probably the result would be an immediate and startling reduction in child mortality, leading to further legislation increasing the quantity of brandy to a gallon. Not until the brandy craze had been carried to a point at which the direct harm done by it would outweigh the incidental good, would an anti-brandy party be listened to. That incidental good would be the substitution of attention to the general health of children for the neglect which is now the rule so long as the child is not actually too sick to run about and play as usual. Even if this attention were confined to the children's teeth, there would be an improvement which it would take a good deal of brandy to cancel.

This imaginary case explains the actual case of the sanitary appliances which our local sanitary authorities prescribe today and condemn tomorrow. No sanitary contrivance which the mind of even the very worst plumber can devize could be as disastrous as that total neglect for long periods which gets avenged by pestilences that sweep through whole continents, like the black death and the cholera. If it were proposed at this time of day to discharge all the sewage of London crude and untreated into the Thames, instead of carrying it, after elaborate treatment, far out into the North Sea, there would be a shriek of horror from all our experts. Yet if Cromwell had done that instead of doing nothing, there would probably have been no Great Plague of London. When the Local Health Authority forces every householder to have his sanitary arrangements thought about and attended to by somebody whose special business it is to attend to such things, then it matters not how erroneous or even directly mischievous may be the specific measures taken: the net result at first is sure to be an improvement. Not until attention has been effectually substituted for neglect as the general rule, will the statistics begin to shew the merits of the particular methods of attention adopted. And as we are far from having arrived at this stage, being as to health legislation only at the beginning of things, we have practically no evidence yet as to the value of methods. Simple and obvious as this is, nobody seems as yet to discount the effect of substituting attention for neglect in drawing conclusions from health statistics. Everything is put to the credit of the particular method employed, although it may quite possibly be raising the death-rate by five per thousand whilst the attention incidental to it is reducing the death-rate fifteen per thousand. The net gain to ten per thousand is credited to the method, and made the excuse for enforcing more of it.

STEALING CREDIT FROM CIVILIZATION

There is yet another way in which specifics which have no merits at all, either direct or incidental, may be brought into high repute by statistics. For a century past civilization has been cleaning away the conditions which favor bacterial fevers. Typhus, once rife, has vanished: plague and cholera have been stopped at our frontiers by a sanitary blockade. We still have epidemics of smallpox and typhoid; and diphtheria and scarlet fever are endemic in the slums. Measles, which in my childhood was not regarded as a dangerous disease, has now become so mortal that notices are posted publicly urging parents to take it seriously. But even in these cases the contrast between the death and recovery rates in the rich districts and in the poor ones has led to the general conviction among experts that bacterial diseases are preventible; and they already are to a large extent prevented. The dangers of infection and the way to avoid it are better understood than they used to be. It is barely twenty years since people exposed themselves recklessly to the infection of consumption and pneumonia in the belief that these diseases were not "catching." Nowadays the troubles of consumptive patients are greatly increased by the growing disposition to treat them as lepers. No doubt there is a good

deal of ignorant exaggeration and cowardly refusal to face
a human and necessary share of the risk. That has always
been the case. We now know that the medieval horror of
leprosy was out of all proportion to the danger of infection,
and was accompanied by apparent blindness to the infec-
tiousness of smallpox, which has since been worked up by
our disease terrorists into the position formerly held by
leprosy. But the scare of infection, though it sets even doctors talking as if the only really scientific thing to do with
a fever patient is to throw him into the nearest ditch and
pump carbolic acid on him from a safe distance until he is
ready to be cremated on the spot, has led to much greater
care and cleanliness. And the net result has been a series of
victories over disease.

Now let us suppose that in the early nineteenth century
somebody had come forward with a theory that typhus fever
always begins at the top joint of the little finger; and that
if this joint be amputated immediately after birth, typhus
fever will disappear. Had such a suggestion been adopted,
the theory would have been triumphantly confirmed; for
as a matter of fact, typhus fever *has* disappeared. On the
other hand cancer and madness have increased (statistically)
to an appalling extent. The opponents of the little finger
theory would therefore be pretty sure to allege that the
amputations were spreading cancer and lunacy. The vaccination controversy is full of such contentions. So is the
controversy as to the docking of horses' tails and the cropping of dogs' ears. So is the less widely known controversy
as to circumcision and the declaring certain kinds of flesh
unclean by the Jews. To advertize any remedy or operation, you have only to pick out all the most reassuring ad-
vances made by civilization, and boldly present the two in
the relation of cause and effect: the public will swallow the
fallacy without a wry face. It has no idea of the need for
what is called a control experiment. In Shakespear's time
and for long after it, mummy was a favorite medicament.
You took a pinch of the dust of a dead Egyptian in a pint

57

of the hottest water you could bear to drink; and it did you a great deal of good. This, you thought, proved what a sovereign healer mummy was. But if you had tried the control experiment of taking the hot water without the mummy, you might have found the effect exactly the same, and that any hot drink would have done as well.

BIOMETRIKA

Another difficulty about statistics is the technical difficulty of calculation. Before you can even make a mistake in drawing your conclusion from the correlations established by your statistics you must ascertain the correlations. When I turn over the pages of Biometrika, a quarterly journal in which is recorded the work done in the field of biological statistics by Professor Karl Pearson and his colleagues, I am out of my depth at the first line, because mathematics are to me only a concept: I never used a logarithm in my life, and could not undertake to extract the square root of four without misgiving. I am therefore unable to deny that the statistical ascertainment of the correlations between one thing and another must be a very complicated and difficult technical business, not to be tackled successfully except by high mathematicians; and I cannot resist Professor Karl Pearson's immense contempt for, and indignant sense of grave social danger in, the unskilled guesses of the ordinary sociologist.

Now the man in the street knows nothing of Biometrika: all he knows is that "you can prove anything by figures," though he forgets this the moment figures are used to prove anything he wants to believe. If he did take in Biometrika he would probably become abjectly credulous as to all the conclusions drawn in it from the correlations so learnedly worked out; though the mathematician whose correlations would fill a Newton with admiration, may, in collecting and accepting data and drawing conclusions from them, fall into quite crude errors by just such popular oversights as I have been describing.

PREFACE ON DOCTORS
PATIENT-MADE THERAPEUTICS

To all these blunders and ignorances doctors are no less subject than the rest of us. They are not trained in the use of evidence, nor in biometrics, nor in the psychology of human credulity, nor in the incidence of economic pressure. Further, they must believe, on the whole, what their patients believe, just as they must wear the sort of hat their patients wear. The doctor may lay down the law despotically enough to the patient at points where the patient's mind is simply blank; but when the patient has a prejudice the doctor must either keep it in countenance or lose his patient. If people are persuaded that night air is dangerous to health and that fresh air makes them catch cold, it will not be possible for a doctor to make his living in private practice if he prescribes ventilation. We have to go back no further than the days of The Pickwick Papers to find ourselves in a world where people slept in four-post beds with curtains drawn closely round to exclude as much air as possible. Had Mr Pickwick's doctor told him that he would be much healthier if he slept on a camp bed by an open window, Mr Pickwick would have regarded him as a crank and called in another doctor. Had he gone on to forbid Mr Pickwick to drink brandy and water whenever he felt chilly, and assured him that if he were deprived of meat or salt for a whole year, he would not only not die, but would be none the worse, Mr Pickwick would have fled from his presence as from that of a dangerous madman. And in these matters the doctor cannot cheat his patient. If he has no faith in drugs or vaccination, and the patient has, he can cheat him with colored water and pass his lancet through the flame of a spirit lamp before scratching his arm. But he cannot make him change his daily habits without knowing it.

THE REFORMS ALSO COME FROM THE LAITY

In the main, then, the doctor learns that if he gets ahead of the superstitions of his patients he is a ruined man; and the result is that he instinctively takes care not to get ahead of them. That is why all the changes come from the laity. It was not until an agitation had been conducted for many years by laymen, including quacks and faddists of all kinds, that the public was sufficiently impressed to make it possible for the doctors to open their minds and their mouths on the subject of fresh air, cold water, temperance, and the rest of the new fashions in hygiene. At present the tables have been turned on many old prejudices. Plenty of our most popular elderly doctors believe that cold tubs in the morning are unnatural, exhausting, and rheumatic; that fresh air is a fad, and that everybody is the better for a glass or two of port wine every day; but they no longer dare say as much until they know exactly where they are; for many very desirable patients in country houses have lately been persuaded that their first duty is to get up at six in the morning and begin the day by taking a walk barefoot through the dewy grass. He who shews the least scepticism as to this practice is at once suspected of being "an old-fashioned doctor," and dismissed to make room for a younger man.

In short, private medical practice is governed not by science but by supply and demand; and however scientific a treatment may be, it cannot hold its place in the market if there is no demand for it; nor can the grossest quackery be kept off the market if there is a demand for it.

FASHIONS AND EPIDEMICS

A demand, however, can be inculcated. This is thoroughly understood by fashionable tradesmen, who find no difficulty in persuading their customers to renew articles that are not worn out and to buy things they do not want. By making doctors tradesmen, we compel them to learn the tricks of trade; consequently we find that the fashions of the year include treatments, operations, and particular drugs, as well as hats, sleeves, ballads, and games. Tonsils, vermiform appendices, uvulas, even ovaries are sacrificed because it is the fashion to get them cut out, and because the operations are highly profitable. The psychology of

fashion becomes a pathology; for the cases have every air
of being genuine: fashions, after all, are only induced epidemics, proving that epidemics can be induced by tradesmen, and therefore by doctors.

THE DOCTOR'S VIRTUES

It will be admitted that this is a pretty bad state of
things. And the melodramatic instinct of the public, always
demanding that every wrong shall have, not its remedy,
but its villain to be hissed, will blame, not its own apathy,
superstition, and ignorance, but the depravity of the doctors.
Nothing could be more unjust or mischievous. Doctors, if
no better than other men, are certainly no worse. I was re-
proached during the performances of The Doctor's Dilemma at the Court Theatre in 1907 because I made the artist a rascal, the journalist an illiterate incapable, and all the
doctors "angels." But I did not go beyond the warrant of
my own experience. It has been my luck to have doctors
among my friends for nearly forty years past (all perfectly
aware of my freedom from the usual credulity as to the
miraculous powers and knowledge attributed to them); and
though I know that there are medical blackguards as well
as military, legal, and clerical blackguards (one soon finds
that out when one is privileged to hear doctors talking shop
among themselves), the fact that I was no more at a loss for
private medical advice and attendance when I had not a
penny in my pocket than I was later on when I could afford
fees on the highest scale, has made it impossible for me to
share that hostility to the doctor as a man which exists and is
growing as an inevitable result of the present condition of
medical practice. Not that the interest in disease and aberra-
tions which turns some men and women to medicine and
surgery is not sometimes as morbid as the interest in misery
and vice which turns some others to philanthropy and "rescue work." But the true doctor is inspired by a hatred of ill-
health, and a divine impatience of any waste of vital forces.
Unless a man is led to medicine or surgery through a very
exceptional technical aptitude, or because doctoring is a

61

family tradition, or because he regards it unintelligently as a lucrative and gentlemanly profession, his motives in choosing the career of a healer are clearly generous. However actual practice may disillusion and corrupt him, his selection in the first instance is not a selection of a base character.

THE DOCTOR'S HARDSHIPS

A review of the counts in the indictment I have brought against private medical practice will shew that they arise out of the doctor's position as a competitive private tradesman: that is, out of his poverty and dependence. And it should be borne in mind that doctors are expected to treat other people specially well whilst themselves submitting to specially inconsiderate treatment. The butcher and baker are not expected to feed the hungry unless the hungry can pay; but a doctor who allows a fellow-creature to suffer or perish without aid is regarded as a monster. Even if we must dismiss hospital service as really venal, the fact remains that most doctors do a good deal of gratuitous work in private practice all through their careers. And in his paid work the doctor is on a different footing to the tradesman. Although the articles he sells, advice and treatment, are the same for all classes, his fees have to be graduated like the income tax. The successful fashionable doctor may weed his poorer patients out from time to time, and finally use the College of Physicians to place it out of his own power to accept low fees; but the ordinary general practitioner never makes out his bills without considering the taxable capacity of his patients.

Then there is the disregard of his own health and comfort which results from the fact that he is, by the nature of his work, an emergency man. We are polite and considerate to the doctor when there is nothing the matter, and we meet him as a friend or entertain him as a guest; but when the baby is suffering from croup, or its mother has a temperature of 104°, or its grandfather has broken his leg, nobody thinks of the doctor except as a healer and savior. He may

be hungry, weary, sleepy, run down by several successive
nights disturbed by that instrument of torture, the night
bell; but who ever thinks of this in the face of sudden sickness or accident? We think no more of the condition of a
doctor attending a case than of the condition of a fireman at
a fire. In other occupations night-work is specially recognized and provided for. The worker sleeps all day; has his
breakfast in the evening; his lunch or dinner at midnight;
his dinner or supper before going to bed in the morning;
and he changes to day-work if he cannot stand night-work.
But a doctor is expected to work day and night. In practices
which consist largely of workmen's clubs, and in which the
patients are therefore taken on wholesale terms and very
numerous, the unfortunate assistant, or the principal if he
has no assistant, often does not undress, knowing that he
will be called up before he has snatched an hour's sleep. To
the strain of such inhuman conditions must be added the
constant risk of infection. One wonders why the impatient
doctors do not become savage and unmanageable, and the
patient ones imbecile. Perhaps they do, to some extent. And
the pay is wretched, and so uncertain that refusal to attend
without payment in advance becomes often a necessary
measure of self-defence, whilst the County Court has long
ago put an end to the tradition that the doctor's fee is an
honorarium. Even the most eminent physicians, as such
biographies as those of Paget shew, are sometimes miserably, inhumanly poor until they are past their prime.

In short, the doctor needs our help for the moment
much more than we often need his. The ridicule of Molière,
the death of a well-informed and clever writer like the late
Harold Frederic in the hands of Christian Scientists (a sort
of sealing with his blood of the contemptuous disbelief in
and dislike of doctors he had bitterly expressed in his
books), the scathing and quite justifiable exposure of medical practice in the novel by Mr Maarten Maartens entitled
The New Religion: all these trouble the doctor very little,
and are in any case well set off by the popularity of Sir Luke

PREFACE ON DOCTORS

Fildes' famous picture, and by the verdicts in which juries from time to time express their conviction that the doctor can do no wrong. The real woes of the doctor are the shabby coat, the wolf at the door, the tyranny of ignorant patients, the work-day of 24 hours, and the uselessness of honestly prescribing what most of the patients really need: that is, not medicine, but money.

THE PUBLIC DOCTOR

What then is to be done?

Fortunately we have not to begin absolutely from the beginning: we already have, in the Medical Officer of Health, a sort of doctor who is free from the worst hardships, and consequently from the worst vices, of the private practitioner. His position depends, not on the number of people who are ill, and whom he can keep ill, but on the number of people who are well. He is judged, as all doctors and treatments should be judged, by the vital statistics of his district. When the death-rate goes up his credit goes down. As every increase in his salary depends on the issue of a public debate as to the health of the constituency under his charge, he has every inducement to strive towards the ideal of a clean bill of health. He has a safe, dignified, responsible, independent position based wholly on the public health; whereas the private practitioner has a precarious, shabby-genteel, irresponsible, servile position, based wholly on the prevalence of illness.

It is true, there are grave scandals in the public medical service. The public doctor may be also a private practitioner eking out his earnings by giving a little time to public work for a mean payment. There are cases in which the position is one which no successful practitioner will accept, and where, therefore, incapables or drunkards get automatically selected for the post, *faute de mieux*; but even in these cases the doctor is less disastrous in his public capacity than in his private one: besides, the conditions which produce these bad cases are doomed, as the evil is now recognized and understood. A popular but unstable remedy is to enable local au-

64

PREFACE ON DOCTORS

thorities, when they are too small to require the undivided time of such men as the Medical Officers of our great municipalities, to combine for public health purposes so that each may share the services of a highly paid official of the best class; but the right remedy is a larger area as the sanitary unit.

MEDICAL ORGANIZATION

Another advantage of public medical work is that it admits of organization, and consequently of the distribution of the work in such a manner as to avoid wasting the time of highly qualified experts on trivial jobs. The individualism of private practice leads to an appalling waste of time on trifles. Men whose dexterity as operators or almost divinatory skill in diagnosis are constantly needed for difficult cases, are poulticing whitlows, vaccinating, changing unimportant dressings, prescribing ether drams for ladies with timid leanings towards dipsomania, and generally wasting their time in the pursuit of private fees. In no other profession is the practitioner expected to do all the work involved in it from the first day of his professional career to the last as the doctor is. The judge passes sentence of death; but he is not expected to hang the criminal with his own hands, as he would be if the legal profession were as unorganized as the medical. The bishop is not expected to blow the organ or wash the baby he baptizes. The general is not asked to plan a campaign or conduct a battle at half-past twelve and to play the drum at half-past two. Even if they were, things would still not be as bad as in the medical profession; for in it not only is the first-class man set to do third-class work, but, what is much more terrifying, the third-class man is expected to do first-class work. Every general practitioner is supposed to be capable of the whole range of medical and surgical work at a moment's notice; and the country doctor, who has not a specialist nor a crack consultant at the end of his telephone, often has to tackle without hesitation cases which no sane practitioner in a town would take in hand without assistance. No doubt this develops the resourcefulness of the country doctor, and makes him a more capable man than his suburban colleague; but it cannot develop the second-class man into a first-class one. If the practice of law not only led to a judge having to hang, but the hangman to judge, or if in the army matters were so arranged that it would be possible for the drummer boy to be in command at Waterloo whilst the Duke of Wellington was playing the drum in Brussels, we should not be consoled by the reflection that our hangmen were thereby made a little more judicial-minded, and our drummers more responsible, than in foreign countries where the legal and military professions recognized the advantages of division of labor.

Under such conditions no statistics as to the graduation of professional ability among doctors are available. Assuming that doctors are normal men and not magicians (and it is unfortunately very hard to persuade people to admit so much and thereby destroy the romance of doctoring) we may guess that the medical profession, like the other professions, consists of a small percentage of highly gifted persons at one end, and a small percentage of altogether disastrous duffers at the other. Between these extremes comes the main body of doctors (also, of course, with a weak and a strong end) who can be trusted to work under regulations with more or less aid from above according to the gravity of the case. Or, to put it in terms of the cases, there are cases that present no difficulties, and can be dealt with by a nurse or student at one end of the scale, and cases that require watching and handling by the very highest existing skill at the other; whilst between come the great mass of cases which need visits from the doctor of ordinary ability and from the chiefs of the profession in the proportion of, say, seven to none, seven to one, three to one, one to one, or, for a day or two, none to one. Such a service is organized at present only in hospitals; though in large towns the practice of calling in the consultant acts, to some extent, as a substitute for it. But in the latter case it is quite unregulated except by professional etiquet, which, as we have seen, has for its object, not the health of the patient or of the community at large, but the protection of the doctor's livelihood and the concealment of his errors. And as the consultant is an expensive luxury, he is a last resource rather than, as he should be, a matter of course in all cases where the general practitioner is not equal to the occasion: a predicament in which a very capable man may find himself at any time through the cropping up of a case of which he has had no clinical experience.

THE SOCIAL SOLUTION OF THE MEDICAL PROBLEM

The social solution of the medical problem, then, depends on that large, slowly advancing, pettishly resisted integration of society called generally Socialism. Until the medical profession becomes a body of men trained and paid by the country to keep the country in health it will remain what it is at present: a conspiracy to exploit popular credulity and human suffering. Already our M.O.H.s (Medical Officers of Health) are in the new position: what is lacking is appreciation of the change, not only by the public but by the private doctors. For, as we have seen, when one of the first-rate posts becomes vacant in one of the great cities, and all the leading M.O.H.s compete for it, they must appeal to the good health of the cities of which they have been in charge, and not to the size of the incomes the local private doctors are making out of the ill-health of their patients. If a competitor can prove that he has utterly ruined every sort of medical private practice in a large city except obstetric practice and the surgery of accidents, his claims are irresistible; and this is the ideal at which every M.O.H. should aim. But the profession at large should none the less welcome him and set its house in order for the social change which will finally be its own salvation. For the M.O.H. as we know him is only the beginning of that army of Public Hygiene which will presently take the place in general interest and honor now occupied by our military and naval

PREFACE ON DOCTORS

forces. It is silly that an Englishman should be more afraid of a German soldier than of a British disease germ, and should clamor for more barracks in the same newspapers that protest against more school clinics, and cry out that if the State fights disease for us it makes us paupers, though they never say that if the State fights the Germans for us it makes us cowards. Fortunately, when a habit of thought is silly it only needs steady treatment by ridicule from sensible and witty people to be put out of countenance and perish. Every year sees an increase in the number of persons employed in the Public Health Service, who would formerly have been mere adventurers in the Private Illness Service. To put it another way, a host of men and women who have now a strong incentive to be mischievous and even murderous rogues will have a much stronger, because a much honester, incentive to be not only good citizens but active benefactors to the community. And they will have no anxiety whatever about their incomes.

THE FUTURE OF PRIVATE PRACTICE

It must not be hastily concluded that this involves the extinction of the private practitioner. What it will really mean for him is release from his present degrading and scientifically corrupting slavery to his patients. As I have already shewn, the doctor who has to live by pleasing his patients in competition with everybody who has walked the hospitals, scraped through the examinations, and bought a brass plate, soon finds himself prescribing water to teetotallers and brandy or champagne jelly to drunkards; beefsteaks and stout in one house, and "uric acid free" vegetarian diet over the way; shut windows, big fires, and heavy overcoats to old Colonels, and open air and as much nakedness as is compatible with decency to young faddists, never once daring to say either "I dont know," or "I dont agree." For the strength of the doctor's, as of every other man's position when the evolution of social organization at last reaches his profession, will be that he will always have open to him the alternative of public employment when the pri-

68

vate employer becomes too tyrannous. And let no one suppose that the words doctor and patient can disguise from the parties the fact that they are employer and employee. No doubt doctors who are in great demand can be as highhanded and independent as employees are in all classes when a dearth in their labor market makes them indispensable; but the average doctor is not in this position: he is struggling for life in an overcrowded profession, and knows well that "a good bedside manner" will carry him to solvency through a morass of illness, whilst the least attempt at plain dealing with people who are eating too much or drinking too much, or frowsting too much (to go no further in the list of intemperances that make up so much of family life) would soon land him in the Bankruptcy Court.

Private practice, thus protected, would itself protect individuals, as far as such protection is possible, against the errors and superstitions of State medicine, which are at worst no worse than the errors and superstitions of private practice, being, indeed, all derived from it. Such monstrosities as vaccination are, as we have seen, founded, not on science, but on half-crowns. If the Vaccination Acts, instead of being wholly repealed as they are already half repealed, were strengthened by compelling every parent to have his child vaccinated by a public officer whose salary was completely independent of the number of vaccinations performed by him, and for whom there was plenty of alternative public health work waiting, vaccination would be dead in two years, as the vaccinator would not only not gain by it, but would lose credit through the depressing effects on the vital statistics of his district of the illness and deaths it causes, whilst it would take from him all the credit of that freedom from smallpox which is the result of good sanitary administration and vigilant prevention of infection. Such absurd panic scandals as that of the last London epidemic, where a fee of half-a-crown per re-vaccination produced raids on houses during the absence of parents, and the forcible seizure and re-vaccination of children left to answer the

door, can be prevented simply by abolishing the half-crown
and all similar follies, paying, not for this or that ceremony
of witchcraft, but for immunity from disease, and paying,
too, in a rational way. The officer with a fixed salary saves
himself trouble by doing his business with the least possible
interference with the private citizen. The man paid by the
job loses money by not forcing his job on the public as often
as possible without reference to its results.

THE TECHNICAL PROBLEM

As to any technical medical problem specially involved,
there is none. If there were, I should not be competent to
deal with it, as I am not a technical expert in medicine: I
deal with the subject as an economist, a politician, and a
citizen exercising my common sense. Everything that I
have said applies equally to all the medical techniques, and
will hold good whether public hygiene be based on the
poetic fancies of Christian Science, the tribal superstitions of
the druggist and the vivisector, or the best we can make of
our real knowledge. But I may remind those who confus-
edly imagine that the medical problem is also the scientific
problem, that all problems are finally scientific problems.
The notion that therapeutics or hygiene or surgery is any
more or less scientific than making or cleaning boots is entertained only by people to whom a man of science is still a
magician who can cure diseases, transmute metals, and enable us to live for ever. It may still be necessary for some
time to come to practise on popular credulity, popular love
and dread of the marvellous, and popular idolatry, to induce
the poor to comply with the sanitary regulations they are
too ignorant to understand. As I have elsewhere confessed,
I have myself been responsible for ridiculous incantations
with burning sulphur, experimentally proved to be quite
useless, because poor people are convinced, by the mystical
air of the burning and the horrible smell, that it exorcises
the demons of smallpox and scarlet fever and makes it safe
for them to return to their houses. To assure them that the
real secret is sunshine and soap is only to convince them

70

that you do not care whether they live or die, and wish to save money at their expense. So you perform the incantation; and back they go to their houses, satisfied. A religious ceremony—a poetic blessing of the threshold, for instance—would be much better; but unfortunately our religion is weak on the sanitary side. One of the worst misfortunes of Christendom was that reaction against the voluptuous bathing of the imperial Romans which made dirty habits a part of Christian piety, and in some unlucky places (the Sandwich Islands, for example) made the introduction of Christianity also the introduction of disease, because the formulators of the superseded native religion, like Mahomet, had been enlightened enough to introduce as religious duties such sanitary measures as ablution and the most careful and reverent treatment of everything cast off by the human body, even to nail clippings and hairs; and our missionaries thoughtlessly discredited this godly doctrine without supplying its place, which was promptly taken by laziness and neglect. If the priests of Ireland could only be persuaded to teach their flocks that it is a deadly insult to the Blessed Virgin to place her image in a cottage that is not kept up to that high standard of Sunday cleanliness to which all her worshippers must believe she is accustomed, and to represent her as being especially particular about stables because her son was born in one, they might do more in one year than all the Sanitary Inspectors in Ireland could do in twenty; and they could hardly doubt that Our Lady would be delighted. Perhaps they do nowadays; for Ireland is certainly a transfigured country since my youth as far as clean faces and pinafores can transfigure it. In England, where so many of the inhabitants are too gross to believe in poetic faiths, too respectable to tolerate the notion that the stable at Bethany was a common peasant farmer's stable instead of a first-rate racing one, and too savage to believe that anything can really cast out the devil of disease unless it be some terrifying hoodoo of tortures and stinks, the M.O.H. will no doubt for a long time to come have to preach to

71

fools according to their folly, promising miracles, and threatening hideous personal consequences of neglect of by-laws and the like; therefore it will be important that every M.O.H. shall have, with his (or her) other qualifications, a sense of humor, lest he (or she) should come at last to believe all the nonsense that must needs be talked. But he must, in his capacity of an expert advising the authorities, keep the government itself free of superstition. If Italian peasants are so ignorant that the Church can get no hold of them except by miracles, why, miracles there must be. The blood of St Januarius must liquefy whether the Saint is in the humor or not. To trick a heathen into being a dutiful Christian is no worse than to trick a whitewasher into trusting himself in a room where a smallpox patient has lain, by pretending to exorcise the disease with burning sulphur. But woe to the Church if in deceiving the peasant it also deceives itself; for then the Church is lost, and the peasant too, unless he revolt against it. Unless the Church works the pretended miracle painfully against the grain, and is continually urged by its dislike of the imposture to strive to make the peasant susceptible to the true reasons for behaving well, the Church will become an instrument of his corruption and an exploiter of his ignorance, and will find itself launched upon that persecution of scientific truth of which all priesthoods are accused—and none with more justice than the scientific priesthood.

And here we come to the danger that terrifies so many of us: the danger of having a hygienic orthodoxy imposed on us. But we must face that: in such crowded and poverty ridden civilizations as ours any orthodoxy is better than laisser-faire. If our population ever comes to consist exclusively of well-to-do, highly cultivated, and thoroughly instructed free persons in a position to take care of themselves, no doubt they will make short work of a good deal of official regulation that is now of life-and-death necessity to us; but under existing circumstances, I repeat, almost any sort of attention that democracy will stand is better than

Sir Colenso Ridgeon
Raymond Massey

neglect. Attention and activity lead to mistakes as well as to successes; but a life spent in making mistakes is not only more honorable but more useful than a life spent doing nothing. The one lesson that comes out of all our theorizing and experimenting is that there is only one really scientific progressive method; and that is the method of trial and error. If you come to that, what is laisser-faire but an orthodoxy? the most tyrannous and disastrous of all the orthodoxies, since it forbids you even to learn.

THE LATEST THEORIES

Medical theories are so much a matter of fashion, and the most fertile of them are modified so rapidly by medical practice and biological research, which are international activities, that the play which furnishes the pretext for this preface is already slightly outmoded, though I believe it may be taken as a faithful record for the year (1906) in which it was begun. I must not expose any professional man to ruin by connecting his name with the entire freedom of criticism which I, as a layman, enjoy; but it will be evident to all experts that my play could not have been written but for the work done by Sir Almroth Wright in the theory and practice of securing immunization from bacterial diseases by the inoculation of "vaccines" made of their own bacteria: a practice incorrectly called vaccinetherapy (there is nothing vaccine about it) apparently because it is what vaccination ought to be and is not. Until Sir Almroth Wright, following up one of Metchnikoff's most suggestive biological romances, discovered that the white corpuscles or phagocytes which attack and devour disease germs for us do their work only when we butter the disease germs appetizingly for them with a natural sauce which Sir Almroth named opsonin, and that our production of this condiment continually rises and falls rhythmically from negligibility to the highest efficiency, nobody had been able even to conjecture why the various serums that were from time to time introduced as having effected marvellous cures, presently made such direful havoc of some unfor-

73

tunate patient that they had to be dropped hastily. The quantity of sturdy lying that was necessary to save the credit of inoculation in those days was prodigious; and had it not been for the devotion shewn by the military authorities throughout Europe, who would order the entire disappearance of some disease from their armies, and bring it about by the simple plan of changing the name under which the cases were reported, or for our own Metropolitan Asylums Board, which carefully suppressed all the medical reports that revealed the sometimes quite appalling effects of epidemics of revaccination, there is no saying what popular reaction might not have taken place against the whole immunization movement in therapeutics.

The situation was saved when Sir Almroth Wright pointed out that if you inoculated a patient with pathogenic germs at a moment when his powers of cooking them for consumption by the phagocytes was receding to its lowest point, you would certainly make him a good deal worse and perhaps kill him, whereas if you made precisely the same inoculation when the cooking power was rising to one of its periodical climaxes, you would stimulate it to still further exertions and produce just the opposite result. And he invented a technique for ascertaining in which phase the patient happened to be at any given moment. The dramatic possibilities of this discovery and invention will be found in my play. But it is one thing to invent a technique: it is quite another to persuade the medical profession to acquire it. Our general practitioners, I gather, simply declined to acquire it, being mostly unable to afford either the acquisition or the practice of it when acquired. Something simple, cheap, and ready at all times for all comers, is, as I have shewn, the only thing that is economically possible in general practice, whatever may be the case in Sir Almroth's famous laboratory in St Mary's Hospital. It would have become necessary to denounce opsonin in the trade papers as a fad and Sir Almroth as a dangerous man if his practice in the laboratory had not led him to the conclusion that the customary inoculations were very much too powerful, and that a comparatively infinitesimal dose would not precipitate a negative phase of cooking activity, and might induce a positive one. And thus it happens that the refusal of our general practitioners to acquire the new technique is no longer quite so dangerous in practice as it was when The Doctor's Dilemma was written: nay, that Sir Ralph Bloomfield Bonington's way of administering inoculations as if they were spoonfuls of squills may sometimes work fairly well. For all that, I find Sir Almroth Wright, on the 23rd May 1910, warning the Royal Society of Medicine that "the clinician has not yet been prevailed upon to reconsider his position," which means that the general practitioner ("the doctor," as he is called in our homes) is going on just as he did before, and could not afford to learn or practise a new technique even if he had ever heard of it. To the patient who does not know about it he will say nothing. To the patient who does, he will ridicule it, and disparage Sir Almroth. What else can he do, except confess his ignorance and starve?

But now please observe how "the whirligig of time brings its revenges." This latest discovery of the remedial virtue of a very very tiny hair of the dog that bit you reminds us, not only of Arndt's law of protoplasmic reaction to stimuli, according to which weak and strong stimuli provoke opposite reactions, but of Hahnemann's homeopathy, which was founded on the fact alleged by Hahnemann that drugs which produce certain symptoms when taken in ordinary perceptible quantities, will, when taken in infinitesimally small quantities, provoke just the opposite symptoms; so that the drug that gives you a headache will also cure a headache if you take little enough of it. I have already explained that the savage opposition which homeopathy encountered from the medical profession was not a scientific oppositon; for nobody seems to deny that some drugs act in the alleged manner. It was opposed simply because doctors and apothecaries lived by selling bottles

75

and boxes of doctor's stuff to be taken in spoonfuls or in pellets as large as peas; and people would not pay as much for drops and globules no bigger than pins' heads. Nowadays, however, the more cultivated folk are beginning to be so suspicious of drugs, and the incorrigibly superstitious people so profusely supplied with patent medicines (the medical advice to take them being wrapped round the bottle and thrown in for nothing) that homeopathy has become a way of rehabilitating the trade of prescription compounding, and is consequently coming into professional credit. At which point the theory of opsonins comes very opportunely to shake hands with it.

Add to the newly triumphant homeopathist and the opsonist that other remarkable innovator, the Swedish masseur, who does not theorize about you, but probes you all over with his powerful thumbs until he finds out your sore spots and rubs them away, besides cheating you into a little wholesome exercise; and you have nearly everything in medical practice today that is not flat witchcraft or pure commercial exploitation of human credulity and fear of death. Add to them a good deal of vegetarian and teetotal controversy raging round a clamor for scientific eating and drinking, and resulting in little so far except calling digestion Metabolism and dividing the public between the eminent doctor who tells us that we do not eat enough fish, and his equally eminent colleague who warns us that a fish diet must end in leprosy, and you have all that opposes with any sort of countenance the rise of Christian Science with its cathedrals and congregations and zealots and miracles and cures: all very silly, no doubt, but sane and sensible, poetic and hopeful, compared to the pseudo science of the commercial general practitioner, who foolishly clamors for the prosecution and even the execution of the Christian Scientists when their patients die, forgetting the long death roll of his own patients.

By the time this preface is in print the kaleidoscope may have had another shake; and opsonin may have gone the

PREFACE ON DOCTORS

way of phlogiston at the hands of its own restless discoverer.
I will not say that Hahnemann may have gone the way of
Diafoirus; for Diafoirus we have always with us. But we
shall still pick up all our knowledge in pursuit of some
Will o' the Wisp or other. What is called science has always
pursued the Elixir of Life and the Philosopher's Stone, and
is just as busy after them today as ever it was in the days
of Paracelsus. We call them by different names: Immunization or radiotherapy or what not; but the dreams which lure
us into the adventures from which we learn are always at
bottom the same. Science becomes dangerous only when it
imagines that it has reached its goal. What is wrong with
priests and popes is that instead of being apostles and saints,
they are nothing but empirics who say "I know" instead of
"I am learning," and pray for credulity and inertia as wise
men pray for scepticism and activity. Such abominations as
the Inquisition and the Vaccination Acts are possible only
in the famine years of the soul, when the great vital dogmas
of honor, liberty, courage, the kinship of all life, faith that
the unknown is greater than the known and is only the As
Yet Unknown, and resolution to find a manly highway to
it, have been forgotten in a paroxysm of littleness and terror
in which nothing is active except concupiscence and the fear
of death, playing on which any trader can filch a fortune,
any blackguard gratify his cruelty, and any tyrant make us
his slaves.

Lest this should seem too rhetorical a conclusion for our
professional men of science, who are mostly trained not to
believe anything unless it is worded in the jargon of those
writers who, because they never really understand what
they are trying to say, cannot find familiar words for it, and
are therefore compelled to invent a new language of nonsense for every book they write, let me sum up my conclusions as dryly as is consistent with accurate thought and live
conviction.

1. Nothing is more dangerous than a poor doctor: not
even a poor employer or a poor landlord.

PREFACE ON DOCTORS

2. Of all the anti-social vested interests the worst is the vested interest in ill-health.

3. Remember that an illness is a misdemeanor; and treat the doctor as an accessory unless he notifies every case to the Public Health Authority.

4. Treat every death as a possible and, under our present system, a probable murder, by making it the subject of a reasonably conducted inquest; and execute the doctor, if necessary, *as* a doctor, by striking him off the register.

5. Make up your mind how many doctors the community needs to keep it well. Do not register more or less than this number; and let registration constitute the doctor a civil servant with a dignified living wage paid out of public funds.

6. Municipalize Harley Street.

7. Treat the private operator exactly as you would treat a private executioner.

8. Treat persons who profess to be able to cure disease as you treat fortune tellers.

9. Keep the public carefully informed, by special statistics and announcements of individual cases, of all illnesses of doctors or in their families.

10. Make it compulsory for a doctor using a brass plate to have inscribed on it, in addition to the letters indicating his qualifications, the words "Remember that I too am mortal."

11. In legislation and social organization, proceed on the principle that invalids, meaning persons who cannot keep themselves alive by their own activities, cannot, beyond reason, expect to be kept alive by the activity of others. There is a point at which the most energetic policeman or doctor, when called upon to deal with an apparently drowned person, gives up artificial respiration, although it is never possible to declare with certainty, at any point short of decomposition, that another five minutes of the exercise would not effect resuscitation. The theory that every individual alive is of infinite value is legislatively

78

impracticable. No doubt the higher the life we secure to the individual by wise social organization, the greater his value is to the community, and the more pains we shall take to pull him through any temporary danger or disablement. But the man who costs more than he is worth is doomed by sound hygiene as inexorably as by sound economics.

12. Do not try to live for ever. You will not succeed.

13. Use your health, even to the point of wearing it out. That is what it is for. Spend all you have before you die; and do not outlive yourself.

14. Take the utmost care to get well born and well brought up. This means that your mother must have a good doctor. Be careful to go to a school where there is what they call a school clinic, where your nutrition and teeth and eyesight and other matters of importance to you will be attended to. Be particularly careful to have all this done at the expense of the nation, as otherwise it will not be done at all, the chances being about forty to one against your being able to pay for it directly yourself, even if you know how to set about it. Otherwise you will be what most people are at present: an unsound citizen of an unsound nation, without sense enough to be ashamed or unhappy about it.

1911.

POSTSCRIPT, 1930. During the years which have elapsed since the foregoing preface was penned, the need for bringing the medical profession under responsible and effective public control has become constantly more pressing as the inevitable collisions between the march of discovery in therapeutic science and the reactionary obsolescence of the General Medical Council have become more frequent and sensational. A later volume in the present edition of my works deals with this development.

G. B. S.

79

THE DOCTOR'S DILEMMA
1906

I am grateful to Hesba Stretton, the authoress of "Jessica's First Prayer," for permission to use the title of one of her stories for this play.

ACT I

ON the 15th June 1903, in the early forenoon, a medical student, surname Redpenny, Christian name unknown and of no importance, sits at work in a doctor's consulting-room. He devils for the doctor by answering his letters, acting as his domestic laboratory assistant, and making himself indispensable generally, in return for unspecified advantages involved by intimate intercourse with a leader of his profession, and amounting to an informal apprenticeship and a temporary affiliation. Redpenny is not proud, and will do anything he is asked without reservation of his personal dignity if he is asked in a fellow-creaturely way. He is a wide-open-eyed, ready, credulous, friendly, hasty youth, with his hair and clothes in reluctant transition from the untidy boy to the tidy doctor.

Redpenny is interrupted by the entrance of an old serving-woman who has never known the cares, the preoccupations, the responsibilities, jealousies, and anxieties of personal beauty. She has the complexion of a never-washed gypsy, incurable by any detergent; and she has, not a regular beard and moustaches, which could at least be trimmed and waxed into a masculine presentableness, but a whole crop of small beards and moustaches, mostly springing from moles all over her face. She carries a duster and toddles about meddlesomely, spying out dust so diligently that whilst she is flicking off one speck she is already looking elsewhere for another. In conversation she has the same trick, hardly ever looking at the person she is addressing except when she is excited. She has only one manner, and that is the manner of an old family nurse to a child just after it has learnt to walk. She has used her ugliness to secure indulgences unattainable by Cleopatra or Fair Rosamund, and has the further great advantage over them that age increases her qualification instead of impairing it. Being an industrious, agreeable, and popular old soul, she is a walking sermon on the vanity of feminine

83

prettiness. Just as Redpenny has no discovered Christian name, she has no discovered surname, and is known throughout the doctors' quarter between Cavendish Square and the Marylebone Road simply as Emmy.

The consulting-room has two windows looking on Queen Anne Street. Between the two is a marble-topped console, with haunched gilt legs ending in sphinx claws. The huge pier-glass which surmounts it is mostly disabled from reflection by elaborate painting on its surface of palms, ferns, lilies, tulips, and sunflowers. The adjoining wall contains the fireplace, with two arm-chairs before it. As we happen to face the corner we see nothing of the other two walls. On the right of the fireplace, or rather on the right of any person facing the fireplace, is the door. On its left is the writing-table at which Redpenny sits. It is an untidy table with a microscope, several test tubes, and a spirit lamp standing up through its litter of papers. There is a couch in the middle of the room, at right angles to the console, and parallel to the fireplace. A chair stands between the couch and the windowed wall. The windows have green Venetian blinds and rep curtains; and there is a gasalier; but it is a convert to electric lighting. The wall paper and carpets are mostly green, coeval with the gasalier and the Venetian blinds. The house, in fact, was so well furnished in the middle of the XIXth century that it stands unaltered to this day and is still quite presentable.

EMMY [*entering and immediately beginning to dust the couch*] Theres a lady bothering me to see the doctor.

REDPENNY [*distracted by the interruption*] Well, she cant see the doctor. Look here: whats the use of telling you that the doctor cant take any new patients, when the moment a knock comes to the door, in you bounce to ask whether he can see somebody?

EMMY. Who asked you whether he could see somebody?

REDPENNY. You did.

EMMY. I said theres a lady bothering me to see the doctor. That isnt asking. Its telling.

REDPENNY. Well, is the lady bothering you any reason for you to come bothering me when I'm busy?

EMMY. Have you seen the papers?

REDPENNY. No.

EMMY. Not seen the birthday honors?

REDPENNY [*beginning to swear*] What the—

.EMMY. Now, now, ducky!

REDPENNY. What do you suppose I care about the birthday honors? Get out of this with your chattering. Dr Ridgeon will be down before I have these letters ready. Get out.

EMMY. Dr Ridgeon wont never be down any more, young man.

She detects dust on the console and is down on it immediately.

REDPENNY [*jumping up and following her*] What?

EMMY. He's been made a knight. Mind you dont go Dr Ridgeoning him in them letters. Sir Colenso Ridgeon is to be his name now.

REDPENNY. I'm jolly glad.

EMMY. I never was so taken aback. I always thought his great discoveries was fudge (let alone the mess of them) with his drops of blood and tubes full of Maltese fever and the like. Now he'll have a rare laugh at me.

REDPENNY. Serve you right! It was like your cheek to talk to him about science. [*He returns to his table and resumes his writing*].

EMMY. Oh, I dont think much of science; and neither will you when youve lived as long with it as I have. Whats on my mind is answering the door. Old Sir Patrick Cullen has been here already and left first congratulations—hadnt time to come up on his way to the hospital, but was determined to be first—coming back, he said. All the rest will be here too: the knocker will be going all day. What I'm afraid of is that the doctor'll want a footman like all the rest, now that he's Sir Colenso. Mind: dont you go putting him up to it, ducky; for he'll never have any comfort with anybody but me to answer the door. I know who to let in and who to keep out. And that reminds me of the poor lady. I think he ought to see her. She's just the kind that puts him in a good temper. [*She dusts Redpenny's papers*].

REDPENNY. I tell you he cant see anybody. Do go away, Emmy. How can I work with you dusting all over me like this?

EMMY. I'm not hindering you working—if you call writing letters working. There goes the bell. [*She looks out of the window*]. A doctor's carriage. Thats more congratulations. [*She is going out when Sir Colenso Ridgeon enters*]. Have you finished your two eggs, sonny?

RIDGEON. Yes.

EMMY. Have you put on your clean vest?

RIDGEON. Yes.

EMMY. Thats my ducky diamond! Now keep yourself tidy and dont go messing about and dirtying your hands: the people are coming to congratulate you. [*She goes out*].

Sir Colenso Ridgeon is a man of fifty who has never shaken off his youth. He has the off-handed manner and the little audacities of address which a shy and sensitive man acquires in breaking himself in to intercourse with all sorts and conditions of men. His face is a good deal lined; his movements are slower than, for instance, Redpenny's; and his flaxen hair has lost its lustre; but in figure and manner he is more the young man than the titled physician. Even the lines in his face are those of overwork and restless scepticism, perhaps partly of curiosity and appetite, rather than of age. Just at present the announcement of his knighthood in the morning papers makes him specially self-conscious, and consequently specially off-hand with Redpenny.

RIDGEON. Have you seen the papers? Youll have to

86

THE DOCTOR'S DILEMMA

alter the name in the letters if you havnt.

REDPENNY. Emmy has just told me. I'm awfully glad. I—

RIDGEON. Enough, young man, enough. You will soon get accustomed to it.

REDPENNY. They ought to have done it years ago.

RIDGEON. They would have; only they couldnt stand Emmy opening the door, I daresay.

EMMY [*at the door, announcing*] Dr Shoemaker. [*She withdraws*].

A middle-aged gentleman, well dressed, comes in with a friendly but propitiatory air, not quite sure of his reception. His combination of soft manners and responsive kindliness, with a certain unseizable reserve and a familiar yet foreign chiselling of feature, reveal the Jew: in this instance the handsome gentlemanly Jew, gone a little pigeon-breasted and stale after thirty, as handsome young Jews often do, but still decidedly good-looking.

THE GENTLEMAN. Do you remember me? Schutzmacher. University College school and Belsize Avenue. Loony Schutzmacher, you know.

RIDGEON. What! Loony! [*He shakes hands cordially*]. Why, man, I thought you were dead long ago. Sit down. [*Schutzmacher sits on the couch: Ridgeon on the chair between it and the window*]. Where have you been these thirty years?

SCHUTZMACHER. In general practice, until a few months ago. I've retired.

RIDGEON. Well done, Loony! I wish *I* could afford to retire. Was your practice in London?

SCHUTZMACHER. No.

RIDGEON. Fashionable coast practice, I suppose.

SCHUTZMACHER. How could I afford to buy a fashionable practice? I hadnt a rap. I set up in a manufacturing town in the midlands in a little surgery at ten shillings a week.

RIDGEON. And made your fortune?

87

THE DOCTOR'S DILEMMA

SCHUTZMACHER. Well, I'm pretty comfortable. I have a place in Hertfordshire besides our flat in town. If you ever want a quiet Saturday to Monday, I'll take you down in my motor at an hour's notice.

RIDGEON. Just rolling in money! I wish you rich g.p.'s would teach me how to make some. Whats the secret of it?

SCHUTZMACHER. Oh, in my case the secret was simple enough, though I suppose I should have got into trouble if it had attracted any notice. And I'm afraid you'll think it rather infra dig.

RIDGEON. Oh, I have an open mind. What was the secret?

SCHUTZMACHER. Well, the secret was just two words.

RIDGEON. Not Consultation Free, was it?

SCHUTZMACHER [shocked] No, no. Really!

RIDGEON [apologetic] Of course not. I was only joking.

SCHUTZMACHER. My two words were simply Cure Guaranteed.

RIDGEON [admiring] Cure Guaranteed!

SCHUTZMACHER. Guaranteed. After all, thats what everybody wants from a doctor, isn't it?

RIDGEON. My dear Loony, it was an inspiration. Was it on the brass plate?

SCHUTZMACHER. There was no brass plate. It was a shop window: red, you know, with black lettering. Doctor Leo Schutzmacher, L.R.C.P.M.R.C.S. Advice and medicine sixpence. Cure Guaranteed.

RIDGEON. And the guarantee proved sound nine times out of ten, eh?

SCHUTZMACHER [rather hurt at so moderate an estimate] Oh, much oftener than that. You see, most people get well all right if they are careful and you give them a little sensible advice. And the medicine really did them good. Parrish's Chemical Food: phosphates, you know. One tablespoonful to a twelve-ounce bottle of water: nothing better, no matter what the case is.

88

For half-a-crown she's had a consultation with . . . Cutler Walpole

Katharine Cornell and Ralph Forbes

THE DOCTOR'S DILEMMA

RIDGEON. Redpenny: make a note of Parrish's Chemical Food.

SCHUTZMACHER. I take it myself, you know, when I feel run down. Good-bye. You dont mind my calling, do you? Just to congratulate you.

RIDGEON. Delighted, my dear Loony. Come to lunch on Saturday next week. Bring your motor and take me down to Hertford.

SCHUTZMACHER. I will. We shall be delighted. Thank you. Good-bye. [*He goes out with Ridgeon, who returns immediately*].

REDPENNY. Old Paddy Cullen was here before you were up, to be the first to congratulate you.

RIDGEON. Indeed. Who taught you to speak of Sir Patrick Cullen as old Paddy Cullen, you young ruffian?

REDPENNY. You never call him anything else.

RIDGEON. Not now that I am Sir Colenso. Next thing, you fellows will be calling me old Colly Ridgeon.

REDPENNY. We do, at St Anne's.

RIDGEON. Yach! Thats what makes the medical student the most disgusting figure in modern civilization. No veneration, no manners—no—

EMMY [*at the door, announcing*] Sir Patrick Cullen. [*She retires*].

Sir Patrick Cullen is more than twenty years older than Ridgeon, not yet quite at the end of his tether, but near it and resigned to it. His name, his plain, downright, sometimes rather arid common sense, his large build and stature, the absence of those odd moments of ceremonial servility by which an old English doctor sometimes shews you what the status of the profession was in England in his youth, and an occasional turn of speech, are Irish; but he has lived all his life in England and is thoroughly acclimatized. His manner to Ridgeon, who he likes, is whimsical and fatherly: to others he is a little gruff and uninviting, apt to substitute more or less expressive grunts for articulate

89

THE DOCTOR'S DILEMMA

speech, and generally indisposed, at his age, to make much social effort. He shakes Ridgeon's hand and beams at him cordially and jocularly.

SIR PATRICK. Well, young chap. Is your hat too small for you, eh?

RIDGEON. Much too small. I owe it all to you.

SIR PATRICK. Blarney, my boy. Thank you all the same. [*He sits in one of the arm-chairs near the fireplace. Ridgeon sits on the couch*]. Ive come to talk to you a bit. [*To Redpenny*] Young man: get out.

REDPENNY. Certainly, Sir Patrick. [*He collects his papers and makes for the door*].

SIR PATRICK. Thank you. Thats a good lad. [*Redpenny vanishes*]. They all put up with me, these young chaps, because I'm an old man, a real old man, not like you. Youre only beginning to give yourself the airs of age. Did you ever see a boy cultivating a moustache? Well, a middle-aged doctor cultivating a grey head is much the same sort of spectacle.

RIDGEON. Good Lord! yes: I suppose so. And I thought that the days of my vanity were past. Tell me: at what age does a man leave off being a fool?

SIR PATRICK. Remember the Frenchman who asked his grandmother at what age we get free from the temptations of love. The old woman said she didn't know. [*Ridgeon laughs*]. Well, I make you the same answer. But the world's growing very interesting to me now, Colly.

RIDGEON. You keep up your interest in science, do you?

SIR PATRICK. Lord! yes. Modern science is a wonderful thing. Look at your great discovery! Look at all the great discoveries! Where are they leading to? Why, right back to my poor dear old father's ideas and discoveries. He's been dead now over forty years. Oh, it's very interesting.

RIDGEON. Well, theres nothing like progress, is there?

SIR PATRICK. Dont misunderstand me, my boy. I'm not belittling your discovery. Most discoveries are made regularly every fifteen years; and it's fully a hundred and fifty

90

since yours was made last. Thats something to be proud of. But your discovery's not new. It's only inoculation. My father practised inoculation until it was made criminal in eighteen-forty. That broke the poor old man's heart, Colly: he died of it. And now it turns out that my father was right after all. Youve brought us back to inoculation.

RIDGEON. I know nothing about smallpox. My line is tuberculosis and typhoid and plague. But of course the principle of all vaccines is the same.

SIR PATRICK. Tuberculosis? M-m-m-m! You've found out how to cure consumption, eh?

RIDGEON. I believe so.

SIR PATRICK. Ah yes. It's very interesting. What is it the old cardinal says in Browning's play? "I have known four and twenty leaders of revolt." Well, I've known over thirty men and found out how to cure consumption. Why do people go on dying of it, Colly? Devilment, I suppose. There was my father's old friend George Boddington of Sutton Coldfield. He discovered the open-air cure in eighteen-forty. He was ruined and driven out of his practice for only opening the windows; and now we wont let a consumptive patient have as much as a roof over his head. Oh, it's very v e r y interesting to an old man.

RIDGEON. You old cynic, you dont believe a bit in my discovery.

SIR PATRICK. No, no: I dont go quite so far as that, Colly. But still, you remember Jane Marsh?

RIDGEON. Jane Marsh? No.

SIR PATRICK. You dont!

RIDGEON. No.

SIR PATRICK. You mean to tell me you dont remember the woman with the tuberculosus ulcer on her arm?

RIDGEON [enlightened] Oh, your washerwoman's daughter. Was her name Jane Marsh? I forgot.

SIR PATRICK. Perhaps youve forgotten also that you undertook to cure her with Koch's tuberculin.

RIDGEON. And instead of curing her, it rotted her arm

right off. Yes: I remember. Poor Jane! However, she makes a good living out of that arm now by shewing it at medical lectures.

SIR PATRICK. Still, that wasnt quite what you intended, was it?

RIDGEON. I took my chance of it.

SIR PATRICK. Jane did, you mean.

RIDGEON. Well, it's always the patient who has to take the chance when an experiment is necessary. And we can find out nothing without experiment.

SIR PATRICK. What did you find out from Jane's case?

RIDGEON. I found out that the inoculation that ought to cure sometimes kills.

SIR PATRICK. I could have told you that. Ive tried these modern inoculations a bit myself. Ive killed people with them; and Ive cured people with them; but I gave them up because I never could tell which I was going to do.

RIDGEON [*taking a pamphlet from a drawer in the writing-table and handing it to him*] Read that the next time you have an hour to spare; and youll find out why.

SIR PATRICK [*grumbling and fumbling for his spectacles*] Oh, bother your pamphlets. Whats the practice of it? [*Looking at the pamphlet*] Opsonin? What the devil is opsonin?

RIDGEON. Opsonin is what you butter the disease germs with to make your white blood corpuscles eat them. [*He sits down again on the couch*].

SIR PATRICK. Thats not new. Ive heard this notion that the white corpuscles—what is it that whats his name?—Metchnikoff—calls them?

RIDGEON. Phagocytes.

SIR PATRICK. Aye, phagocytes: yes, yes, yes. Well, I heard this theory that the phagocytes eat up the disease germs years ago: long before you came into fashion. Besides, they dont always eat them.

RIDGEON. They do when you butter them with opsonin.

SIR PATRICK. Gammon.

THE DOCTOR'S DILEMMA

RIDGEON. No: it's not gammon. What it comes to in practice is this. The phagocytes wont eat the microbes unless the microbes are nicely buttered for them. Well, the patient manufactures the butter for himself all right; but my discovery is that the manufacture of that butter, which I call opsonin, goes on in the system by ups and downs—Nature being always rhythmical, you know—and that what the inoculation does is to stimulate the ups or downs, as the case may be. If we had inoculated Jane Marsh when her butter factory was on the up-grade, we should have cured her arm. But we got in on the down-grade and lost her arm for her. I call the up-grade the positive phase and the down-grade the negative phase. Everything depends on your inoculating at the right moment. Inoculate when the patient is in the negative phase and you kill: inoculate when the patient is in the positive phase and you cure.

SIR PATRICK. And pray how are you to know whether the patient is in the positive or the negative phase?

RIDGEON. Send a drop of the patient's blood to the laboratory at St Anne's; and in fifteen minutes I'll give you his opsonin index in figures. If the figure is one, inoculate and cure: if it's under point eight, inoculate and kill. Thats my discovery: the most important that has been made since Harvey discovered the circulation of the blood. My tuberculosis patients dont die now.

SIR PATRICK. And mine do when my inoculation catches them in the negative phase, as you call it. Eh?

RIDGEON. Precisely. To inject a vaccine into a patient without first testing his opsonin is as near murder as a respectable practitioner can get. If I wanted to kill a man I should kill him that way.

EMMY [looking in] Will you see a lady that wants her husband's lungs cured?

RIDGEON [impatiently] No. Havnt I told you I will see nobody? [To Sir Patrick] I live in a state of siege ever since it got about that I'm a magician who can cure consumption with a drop of serum. [To Emmy] Dont come to me again

93

about people who have no appointments. I tell you I can see nobody.

EMMY. Well, I'll tell her to wait a bit.

RIDGEON [*furious*] Youll tell her I cant see her, and send her away: do you hear?

EMMY [*unmoved*] Well, will you see Mr Cutler Walpole? He dont want a cure: he only wants to congratulate you.

RIDGEON. Of course. Shew him up. [*She turns to go*]. Stop. [*To Sir Patrick*] I want two minutes more with you between ourselves. [*To Emmy*] Emmy: ask Mr. Walpole to wait just two minutes, while I finish a consultation.

EMMY. Oh, h e' l l wait all right. He's talking to the poor lady. [*She goes out*].

SIR PATRICK. Well? what is it?

RIDGEON. Dont laugh at me. I want your advice.

SIR PATRICK. Professional advice?

RIDGEON. Yes. Theres something the matter with me. I dont know what it is.

SIR PATRICK. Neither do I. I suppose youve been sounded.

RIDGEON. Yes, of course. Theres nothing wrong with any of the organs: nothing special, anyhow. But I have a curious aching: I dont know where: I cant localize it. Sometimes I think it's my heart: sometimes I suspect my spine. It doesn't exactly hurt me; but it unsettles me completely. I feel that something is going to happen. And there are other symptoms. Scraps of tunes come into my head that seem to me very pretty, though theyre quite commonplace.

SIR PATRICK. Do you hear voices?

RIDGEON. No.

SIR PATRICK. I'm glad of that. When my patients tell me that theyve made a greater discovery than Harvey, and that they hear voices, I lock them up.

RIDGEON. You think I'm mad! Thats just the suspicion that has come across me once or twice. Tell me the truth: I can bear it.

SIR PATRICK. Youre sure there are no voices?

RIDGEON. Quite sure.

SIR PATRICK. Then it's only foolishness.

RIDGEON. Have you ever met anything like it before in your practice?

SIR PATRICK. Oh, yes: often. It's very common between the ages of seventeen and twenty-two. It sometimes comes on again at forty or thereabouts. Youre a bachelor, you see. It's not serious—if youre careful.

RIDGEON. About my food?

SIR PATRICK. No: about your behavior. Theres nothing wrong with your spine; and theres nothing wrong with your heart; but theres something wrong with your common sense. Youre not going to die; but you may be going to make a fool of yourself. So be careful.

RIDGEON. I see you dont believe in my discovery. Well, sometimes I dont believe in it myself. Thank you all the same. Shall we have Walpole up?

SIR PATRICK. Oh, have him up. [*Ridgeon rings*]. He's a clever operator, is Walpole, though he's only one of your chloroform surgeons. In my early days, you made your man drunk; and the porters and the students held him down; and you had to set your teeth and finish the job fast. Nowadays you work at your ease; and the pain doesn't come until afterwards, when youve taken your cheque and rolled up your bag and left the house. I tell you, Colly, chloroform has done a lot of mischief. It's enabled every fool to be a surgeon.

RIDGEON [*to Emmy, who answers the bell*] Shew Mr Walpole up.

EMMY. He's talking to the lady.

RIDGEON [*exasperated*] Did I not tell you—

Emmy goes out without heeding him. He gives it up, with a shrug, and plants himself with his back to the console, leaning resignedly against it.

SIR PATRICK. I know your Cutler Walpoles and their like. Theyve found out that a man's body's full of bits and

95

scraps of old organs he has no mortal use for. Thanks to chloroform, you can cut half a dozen of them out without leaving him any the worse, except for the illness and the guineas it costs him. I knew the Walpoles well fifteen years ago. The father used to snip off the ends of people's uvulas for fifty guineas, and paint throats with caustic every day for a year at two guineas a time. His brother-in-law extirpated tonsils for two hundred guineas until he took up women's cases at double the fees. Cutler himself worked hard at anatomy to find something fresh to operate on; and at last he got hold of something he calls the nuciform sac, which he's made quite the fashion. People pay him five hundred guineas to cut it out. They might as well get their hair cut for all the difference it makes; but I suppose they feel important after it. You cant go out to dinner now without your neighbor bragging to you of some useless operation or other.

EMMY [*announcing*] Mr Cutler Walpole. [*She goes out*].

Cutler Walpole is an energetic, unhesitating man of forty, with a cleanly modelled face, very decisive and symmetrical about the shortish, salient, rather pretty nose, and the three trimly turned corners made by his chin and jaws. In comparison with Ridgeon's delicate broken lines, and Sir Patrick's softly rugged aged ones, his face looks machine-made and beeswaxed; but his scrutinizing, daring eyes give it life and force. He seems never at a loss, never in doubt: one feels that if he made a mistake he would make it thoroughly and firmly. He has neat, well-nourished hands, short arms, and is built for strength and compactness rather than for height. He is smartly dressed with a fancy waist-coat, a richly colored scarf secured by a handsome ring, ornaments on his watch chain, spats on his shoes, and a general air of the well-to-do sportsman about him. He goes straight across to Ridgeon and shakes hands with him.

WALPOLE. My dear Ridgeon, best wishes! heartiest congratulations! You deserve it.

THE DOCTOR'S DILEMMA

RIDGEON. Thank you.

WALPOLE. As a man, mind you. You deserve it as a man. The opsonin is simple rot, as any capable surgeon can tell you; but we're all delighted to see your personal qualities officially recognized. Sir Patrick: how are you? I sent you a paper lately about a little thing I invented: a new saw. For shoulder blades.

SIR PATRICK [*meditatively*] Yes: I got it. It's a good saw: a useful, handy instrument.

WALPOLE [*confidently*] I knew youd see its points.

SIR PATRICK. Yes: I remember that saw sixty-five years ago.

WALPOLE. What!

SIR PATRICK. It was called a cabinetmaker's jimmy then.

WALPOLE. Get out! Nonsense! Cabinetmaker be—

RIDGEON. Never mind him, Walpole. He's jealous.

WALPOLE. By the way, I hope I'm not disturbing you two in anything private.

RIDGEON. No no. Sit down. I was only consulting him. I'm rather out of sorts. Overwork, I suppose.

WALPOLE [*swiftly*] I know whats the matter with you. I can see it in your complexion. I can feel it in the grip of your hand.

RIDGEON. What is it?

WALPOLE. Blood-poisoning.

RIDGEON. Blood-poisoning! Impossible.

WALPOLE. I tell you, blood-poisoning. Ninety-five per cent of the human race suffer from chronic blood-poisoning, and die of it. It's as simple as A.B.C. Your nuciform sac is full of decaying matter—undigested food and waste products—rank ptomaines. Now you take my advice, Ridgeon. Let me cut it out for you. You'll be another man afterwards.

SIR PATRICK. Dont you like him as he is?

WALPOLE. No I dont. I dont like any man who hasnt a healthy circulation. I tell you this: in an intelligently governed country people wouldnt be allowed to go about with nuciform sacs, making themselves centres of infection.

97

The operation ought to be compulsory: it's ten times more important than vaccination.

SIR PATRICK. Have you had your own sac removed, may I ask?

WALPOLE [*triumphantly*] I havnt got one. Look at me! Ive no symptoms. I'm as sound as a bell. About five per cent of the population havnt got any; and I'm one of the five per cent. I'll give you an instance. You know Mrs Jack Foljambe: the smart Mrs Foljambe? I operated at Easter on her sister-in-law, Lady Gorran, and found she had the biggest sac I ever saw: it held about two ounces. Well, Mrs Foljambe had the right spirit—the genuine hygienic instinct. She couldnt stand her sister-in-law being a clean, sound woman, and she simply a whited sepulchre. So she insisted on my operating on her, too. And by George, sir, she hadnt any sac at all. Not a trace! Not a rudiment! ! I was so taken aback—so interested, that I forgot to take the sponges out, and was stitching them up inside her when the nurse missed them. Somehow, I'd made sure she'd have an exceptionally large one. [*He sits down on the couch, squaring his shoulders and shooting his hands out of his cuffs as he sets his knuckles akimbo*].

EMMY [*looking in*] Sir Ralph Bloomfield Bonington.

A long and expectant pause follows this announcement. All look to the door; but there is no Sir Ralph.

RIDGEON [*at last*] Where is he?

EMMY [*looking back*] Drat him, I thought he was following me. He's stayed down to talk to that lady.

RIDGEON [*exploding*] I told you to tell that lady— [EMMY *vanishes*].

WALPOLE [*jumping up again*] Oh, by the way, Ridgeon, that reminds me. Ive been talking to that poor girl. It's her husband; and she thinks it's a case of consumption: the usual wrong diagnosis: these damned general practitioners ought never to be allowed to touch a patient except under the orders of a consultant. She's been describing his symptoms to me; and the case is as plain as a pikestaff: bad

THE DOCTOR'S DILEMMA

blood-poisoning. Now she's poor. She cant afford to have
him operated on. Well, you send him to me: I'll do it for
nothing. Theres room for him in my nursing home. I'll put
him straight, and feed him up and make her happy. I like
making people happy. [*He goes to the chair near the window*].

EMMY [*looking in*] Here he is.

*Sir Ralph Bloomfield Bonington wafts himself into
the room. He is a tall man, with a head like a tall and
slender egg. He has been in his time a slender man; but
now, in his sixth decade, his waistcoat has filled out some-
what. His fair eyebrows arch good-naturedly and un-
critically. He has a most musical voice; his speech is a
perpetual anthem; and he never tires of the sound of it.
He radiates an enormous self-satisfaction, cheering, reassuring, healing by the mere incompatibility of disease or
anxiety with his welcome presence. Even broken bones,
it is said, have been known to unite at the sound of his
voice: he is a born healer, as independent of mere treatment
and skill as any Christian scientist. When he expands into
oratory or scientific exposition, he is as energetic as Walpole; but it is with a bland, voluminous, atmospheric energy, which envelops its subject and its audience, and makes
interruption or inattention impossible, and imposes veneration and credulity on all but the strongest minds. He is
known in the medical world as B. B.; and the envy aroused
by his success in practice is softened by the conviction that he
is, scientifically considered, a colossal humbug: the fact
being that, though he knows just as much (and just as little) as his contemporaries, the qualifications that pass
muster in common men reveal their weakness when hung
on his egregious personality.*

B. B. Aha! Sir Colenso. S i r Colenso, eh? Welcome to
the order of knighthood.

RIDGEON [*shaking hands*] Thank you, B. B.

B. B. What! Sir Patrick! And how are we to-day? a little chilly? a little stiff? but hale and still the cleverest of

99

us all. [*Sir Patrick grunts*]. What! Walpole! the absent-minded beggar: eh?

WALPOLE. What does that mean?

B. B. Have you forgotten the lovely opera singer I sent you to have that growth taken off her vocal cords?

WALPOLE [*springing to his feet*] Great heavens, man, you dont mean to say you sent her for a throat operation!

B. B. [*archly*] Aha! Ha ha! Aha! [*trilling like a lark as he shakes his finger at Walpole*]. You removed her nuciform sac. Well, well! force of habit! force of habit! Never mind, ne-e-e-ver mind. She got back her voice after it, and thinks you the greatest surgeon alive; and so you are, so you are, so you are.

WALPOLE [*in a tragic whisper, intensely serious*] Blood-poisoning. I see. I see. [*He sits down again*].

SIR PATRICK. And how is a certain distinguished family getting on under your care, Sir Ralph?

B. B. Our friend Ridgeon will be gratified to hear that I have tried his opsonin treatment on little Prince Henry with complete success.

RIDGEON [*startled and anxious*] But how——

B. B. [*continuing*] I suspected typhoid: the head gardener's boy had it; so I just called at St Anne's one day and got a tube of your very excellent serum. You were out, unfortunately.

RIDGEON. I hope they explained to you carefully——

B. B. [*waving away the absurd suggestion*] Lord bless you, my dear fellow, I didnt need any explanations. I'd left my wife in the carriage at the door; and I'd no time to be taught my business by your young chaps. I know all about it. Ive handled these anti-toxins ever since they first came out.

RIDGEON. But theyre not anti-toxins; and theyre dangerous unless you use them at the right time.

B. B. Of course they are. Everything is dangerous unless you take it at the right time. An apple at breakfast does you good: an apple at bedtime upsets you for a week. There

100

THE DOCTOR'S DILEMMA

are only two rules for anti-toxins. First, dont be afraid of them: second, inject them a quarter of an hour before meals, three times a day.

RIDGEON [*appalled*] Great heavens, B. B., no, no, no.

B. B. [*sweeping on irresistibly*] Yes, yes, yes, Colly. The proof of the pudding is in the eating, you know. It was an immense success. It acted like magic on the little prince. Up went his temperature; off to bed I packed him; and in a week he was all right again, and absolutely immune from typhoid for the rest of his life. The family were very nice about it: their gratitude was quite touching; but I said they owed it all to you, Ridgeon; and I am glad to think that your knighthood is the result.

RIDGEON. I am deeply obliged to you. [*Overcome, he sits down on the chair near the couch*].

B. B. Not at all, not at all. Your own merit. Come! come! come! dont give way.

RIDGEON. It's nothing. I was a little giddy just now. Overwork, I suppose.

WALPOLE. Blood-poisoning.

B. B. Overwork! Theres no such thing. I do the work of ten men. Am I giddy? No. NO. If youre not well, you have a disease. It may be a slight one; but it's a disease. And what is a disease? The lodgment in the system of a pathogenic germ, and the multiplication of that germ. What is the remedy? A very simple one. Find the germ and kill it.

SIR PATRICK. Suppose theres no germ?

B. B. Impossible, Sir Patrick: there m u s t be a germ: else how could the patient be ill?

SIR PATRICK. Can you shew me the germ of overwork?

B. B. No; but why? Why? Because, my dear Sir Patrick, though the germ is there, it's invisible. Nature has given it no danger signal for us. These germs—these bacilli—are translucent bodies, like glass, like water. To make them visible you must stain them. Well, my dear Paddy, do what you will, some of them wont stain. They wont take cochineal: they wont take methylene blue; they wont take

101

THE DOCTOR'S DILEMMA

gentian violet: they wont take any coloring matter. Consequently, though we know, as scientific men, that they exist, we cannot see them. But can you disprove their existence? Can you conceive the disease existing without them? Can you, for instance, shew me a case of diphtheria without the bacillus?

SIR PATRICK. No; but I'll shew you the same bacillus, without the disease, in your own throat.

B. B. No, not the same, Sir Patrick. It is an entirely different bacillus; only the two are, unfortunately, so exactly alike that you cannot see the difference. You must understand, my dear Sir Patrick, that every one of these interesting little creatures has an imitator. Just as men imitate each other, germs imitate each other. There is the genuine diphtheria bacillus discovered by Lœffler; and there is the pseudo-bacillus, exactly like it, which you could find, as you say, in my own throat.

SIR PATRICK. And how do you tell one from the other?

B. B. Well, obviously, if the bacillus is the genuine Lœffler, you have diphtheria; and if it's the pseudo-bacillus, youre quite well. Nothing simpler. Science is always simple and always profound. It is only the half-truths that are dangerous. Ignorant faddists pick up some superficial information about germs; and they write to the papers and try to discredit science. They dupe and mislead many honest and worthy people. But science has a perfect answer to them on every point.

> A little learning is a dangerous thing;
> Drink deep; or taste not the Pierian spring.

I mean no disrespect to your generation, Sir Patrick: some of you old stagers did marvels through sheer professional intuition and clinical experience; but when I think of the average men of your day, ignorantly bleeding and cupping and purging, and scattering germs over their patients from their clothes and instruments, and contrast all that with the scientific certainty and simplicity of my treatment of the

102

THE DOCTOR'S DILEMMA

little prince the other day, I cant help being proud of my own generation: the men who were trained on the germ theory, the veterans of the great struggle over Evolution in the seventies. We may have our faults; but at least we are men of science. That is why I am taking up your treatment, Ridgeon, and pushing it. It's scientific. [*He sits down on the chair near the couch*].

EMMY [*at the door, announcing*] Dr Blenkinsop.

Dr Blenkinsop is in very different case from the others. He is clearly not a prosperous man. He is flabby and shabby, cheaply fed and cheaply clothed. He has the lines made by a conscience between his eyes, and the lines made by continual money worries all over his face, cut all the deeper as he has seen better days, and hails his well-to-do colleagues as their contemporary and old hospital friend, though even in this he has to struggle with the diffidence of poverty and relegation to the poorer middle class.

RIDGEON. How are you, Blenkinsop?

BLENKINSOP. Ive come to offer my humble congratulations. Oh dear! all the great guns are before me.

B. B. [*patronizing, but charming*] How d'ye do, Blenkinsop? How d'ye do?

BLENKINSOP. And Sir Patrick, too! [*Sir Patrick grunts*].

RIDGEON. Youve met Walpole, of course?

WALPOLE. How d'ye do?

BLENKINSOP. It's the first time Ive had that honor. In my poor little practice there are no chances of meeting you great men. I know nobody but the St Anne's men of my own day. [*To Ridgeon*] And so youre Sir Colenso. How does it feel?

RIDGEON. Foolish at first. Dont take any notice of it.

BLENKINSOP. I'm ashamed to say I havnt a notion what your great discovery is; but I congratulate you all the same for the sake of old times.

B. B. [*shocked*] But, my dear Blenkinsop, you used to be rather keen on science.

BLENKINSOP. Ah, I used to be a lot of things. I used to

103

have two or three decent suits of clothes, and flannels to go
up the river on Sundays. Look at me now: this is my best;
and it must last till Christmas. What can I do? Ive never
opened a book since I was qualified thirty years ago. I used
to read the medical papers at first; but you know how soon
a man drops that; besides, I cant afford them; and what are
they after all but trade papers, full of advertisements? Ive
forgotten all my science: whats the use of my pretending
I havnt? But I have great experience: clinical experience;
and bedside experience is the main thing, isn't it?

B. B. No doubt; always provided, mind you, that you
have a sound scientific theory to correlate your observations
at the bedside. Mere experience by itself is nothing. If I
take my dog to the bedside with me, he sees what I see.
But he learns nothing from it. Why? Because he's not a
scientific dog.

WALPOLE. It amuses me to hear you physicians and
general practitioners talking about clinical experience. What
do you see at the bedside but the outside of the patient?
Well: it isnt his outside thats wrong, except perhaps in skin
cases. What you want is a daily familiarity with people's in-
sides; and that you can only get at the operating table. I
know what I'm talking about: Ive been a surgeon and a
consultant for twenty years; and Ive never known a general practitioner right in his diagnosis yet. Bring them a
perfectly simple case; and they diagnose cancer, and ar-
thritis, and appendicitis, and every other itis, when any
really experienced surgeon can see that it's a plain case of
blood-poisoning.

BLENKINSOP. Ah, it's easy for you gentlemen to talk;
but what would you say if you had my practice? Except for
the workmen's clubs, my patients are all clerks and shop-
men. They darent be ill: they cant afford it. And when
they break down, what can I do for them? Y o u can send
your people to St Moritz or to Egypt, or recommend horse
exercise or motoring or champagne jelly or complete change
and rest for six months. *I* might as well order my people
104

Emmy [*at the door*] "Well, deary: have you got round him?"

Katharine Cornell and Alice B. Cliffe

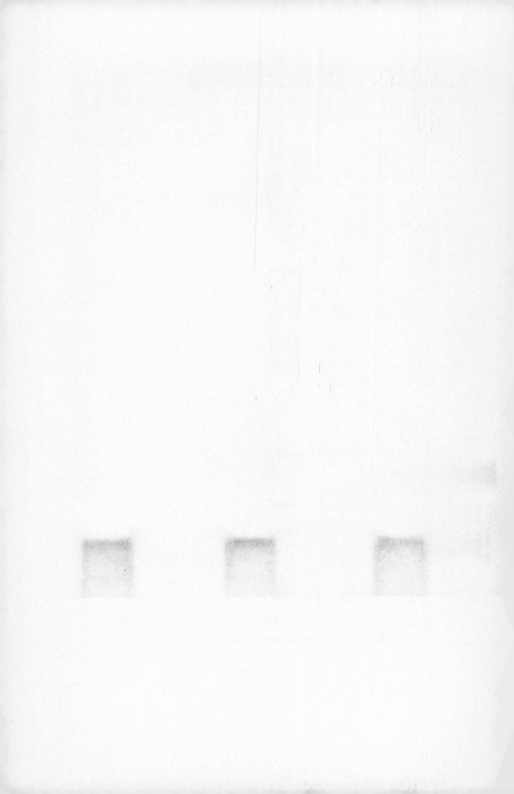

a slice of the moon. And the worst of it is, I'm too poor
to keep well myself on the cooking I have to put up with.
Ive such a wretched digestion; and I look it. How am I
to inspire confidence? [*He sits disconsolately on the
couch*].

RIDGEON. [*restlessly*] Dont, Blenkinsop: it's too painful. The most tragic thing in the world is a sick doctor.

WALPOLE. Yes, by George: its like a bald-headed man
trying to sell a hair restorer. Thank God I'm a surgeon!

B. B. [*sunnily*] I am never sick. Never had a day's illness in my life. Thats what enables me to sympathize with
my patients.

WALPOLE [*interested*] What! youre never ill?

B. B. Never.

WALPOLE. Thats interesting. I believe you have no nuciform sac. If you ever do feel at all queer, I should very
much like to have a look.

B. B. Thank you, my dear fellow; but I'm too busy just
now.

RIDGEON. I was just telling them when you came in,
Blenkinsop, that I have worked myself out of sorts.

BLENKINSOP. Well, it seems presumptuous of me to
offer a prescription to a great man like you; but still I have
great experience; and if I might recommend a pound of
ripe greengages every day half an hour before lunch, I'm
sure youd find a benefit. Theyre very cheap.

RIDGEON. What do you say to that B. B.?

B. B. [*encouragingly*] Very sensible, Blenkinsop: very
sensible indeed. I'm delighted to see that you disapprove
of drugs.

SIR PATRICK [*grunts*]!

B. B. [*archly*] Aha! Haha! Did I hear from the fireside
armchair the bow-wow of the old school defending its
drugs? Ah, believe me, Paddy, the world would be healthier if every chemist's shop in England were demolished.
Look at the papers! full of scandalous advertisements of
patent medicines! a huge commercial system of quackery

and poison. Well, whose fault is it? Ours. I say, ours. We set the example. We spread the superstition. We taught the people to believe in bottles of doctor's stuff; and now they buy it at the stores instead of consulting a medical man.

WALPOLE. Quite true. Ive not prescribed a drug for the last fifteen years.

B. B. Drugs can only repress symptoms: they cannot eradicate disease. The true remedy for all diseases is Nature's remedy. Nature and Science are at one, Sir Patrick, believe me; though you were taught differently. Nature has provided, in the white corpuscles as you call them—in the phagocytes as we call them—a natural means of devouring and destroying all disease germs. There is at bottom only one genuinely scientific treatment for all diseases, and that is to stimulate the phagocytes. Stimulate the phagocytes. Drugs are a delusion. Find the germ of the disease; prepare from it a suitable anti-toxin; inject it three times a day quarter of an hour before meals; and what is the result? The phagocytes are stimulated; they devour the disease; and the patient recovers—unless, of course, he's too far gone. That, I take it, is the essence of Ridgeon's discovery.

SIR PATRICK [dreamily] As I sit here, I seem to hear my poor old father talking again.

B. B. [rising in incredulous amazement] Your father! But, Lord bless my soul, Paddy, your father must have been an older man than you.

SIR PATRICK. Word for word almost, he said what you say. No more drugs. Nothing but inoculation.

B. B. [almost contemptuously] Inoculation! Do you mean smallpox inoculation?

SIR PATRICK. Yes. In the privacy of our family circle, sir, my father used to declare his belief that smallpox inoculation was good, not only for smallpox, but for all fevers.

B. B. [suddenly rising to the new idea with immense interest and excitement] What! Ridgeon: did you hear that? Sir Patrick: I am more struck by what you have just told me than I can well express. Your father, sir, anticipated a

106

discovery of my own. Listen, Walpole. Blenkinsop: attend one moment. You will all be intensely interested in this. I was put on the track by accident. I had a typhoid case and a tetanus case side by side in the hospital: a beadle and a city missionary. Think of what that meant for them, poor fellows! Can a beadle be dignified with typhoid? Can a missionary be eloquent with lockjaw? No. NO. Well, I got some typhoid anti-toxin from Ridgeon and a tube of Muldooley's anti-tetanus serum. But the missionary jerked all my things off the table in one of his paroxysms; and in replacing them I put Ridgeon's tube where Muldooley's ought to have been. The consequence was that I inoculated the typhoid case for tetanus and the tetanus case for typhoid. [*The doctors look greatly concerned. B. B., undamped, smiles triumphantly*]. Well, they recovered. THEY RECOVERED. Except for a touch of St Vitus's dance the missionary's as well to-day as ever; and the beadle's ten times the man he was.

BLENKINSOP. Ive known things like that happen. They cant be explained.

B. B. [*severely*] Blenkinsop: there is n o t h i n g that cannot be explained by science. What did I do? Did I fold my hands helplessly and say that the case could not be explained? By no means. I sat down and used my brains. I thought the case out on scientific principles. I asked myself why didnt the missionary die of typhoid on top of tetanus, and the beadle of tetanus on top of typhoid? Theres a problem for you, Ridgeon. Think, Sir Patrick. Reflect, Blenkinsop. Look at it without prejudice, Walpole. What is the real work of the anti-toxin? Simply to stimulate the phagocytes. Very well. But so long as you stimulate the phagocytes, what does it matter which particular sort of serum you use for the purpose? Haha! Eh? Do you see? Do you grasp it? Ever since that Ive used all sorts of anti-toxins absolutely indiscriminately, with perfectly satisfactory results. I inoculated the little prince with your stuff, Ridgeon, because I wanted to give you a lift; but two years ago I tried

THE DOCTOR'S DILEMMA

the experiment of treating a scarlet fever case with a sample
of hydrophobia serum from the Pasteur Institute, and it
answered capitally. It stimulated the phagocytes; and the
phagocytes did the rest. That is why Sir Patrick's father
found that inoculation cured all fevers. It stimulated the
phagocytes. [*He throws himself into his chair, exhausted
with the triumph of his demonstration, and beams magnif-
icently on them*].

EMMY [*looking in*]. Mr Walpole: your motor's come
for you; and it's frightening Sir Patrick's horses; so come
along quick.

WALPOLE [*rising*] Good-bye, Ridgeon.

RIDGEON. Good-bye; and many thanks.

B. B. You see my point, Walpole?

EMMY. He cant wait, Sir Ralph. The carriage will be
into the area if he dont come.

WALPOLE. I'm coming. [*To B. B.*] Theres nothing in
your point: phagocytosis is pure rot: the cases are all blood-
poisoning; and the knife is the real remedy. Bye-bye, Sir
Paddy. Happy to have met you, Mr. Blenkinsop. Now,
Emmy. [*He goes out, followed by Emmy*].

B. B. [*sadly*] Walpole has no intellect. A mere surgeon.
Wonderful operator; but, after all, what is operating? Only
manual labor. Brain—BRAIN remains master of the situation. The nuciform sac is utter nonsense: theres no such
organ. It's a mere accidental kink in the membrane, oc-
curring in perhaps two-and-a-half per cent of the population. Of course I'm glad for Walpole's sake that the operation is fashionable; for he's a dear good fellow; and after
all, as I always tell people, the operation will do them no
harm: indeed, Ive known the nervous shake-up and the
fortnight in bed do people a lot of good after a hard London
season; but still it's a shocking fraud. [*Rising*] Well, I
must be toddling. Good-bye, Paddy [*Sir Patrick grunts*]
good-bye, good-bye. Good-bye, my dear Blenkinsop, good-
bye! Good-bye, Ridgeon. Dont fret about your health: you
know what to do: if your liver is sluggish, a little mercury

108

never does any harm. If you feel restless, try bromide. If that doesnt answer, a stimulant, you know: a little phosphorus and strychnine. If you cant sleep, trional, trional, trion—

SIR PATRICK [*drily*] But no drugs, Colly, remember that.

. B. B. [*firmly*] Certainly not. Quite right, Sir Patrick. As temporary expedients, of course; but as treatment, no, NO. Keep away from the chemist's shop, my dear Ridgeon, whatever you do.

RIDGEON [*going to the door with him*] I will. And thank you for the knighthood. Good-bye.

B. B. [*stopping at the door, with the beam in his eye twinkling a little*] By the way, who's your patient?

RIDGEON. Who?

B. B. Downstairs. Charming woman. Tuberculous husband.

RIDGEON. Is she there still?

EMMY [*looking in*] Come on, Sir Ralph: your wife's waiting in the carriage.

B. B. [*suddenly sobered*] Oh! Good-bye. [*He goes out almost precipitately*].

RIDGEON. Emmy: is that woman there still? If so, tell her once for all that I cant and wont see her. Do you hear?

EMMY. Oh, she aint in a hurry: she doesnt mind how long she waits. [*She goes out*].

BLENKINSOP. I must be off, too: every half-hour I spend away from my work costs me eighteenpence. Good-bye, Sir Patrick.

SIR PATRICK. Good-bye. Good-bye.

RIDGEON. Come to lunch with me some day this week.

BLENKINSOP. I cant afford it, dear boy; and it would put me off my own food for a week. Thank you all the same.

RIDGEON [*uneasy at Blenkinsop's poverty*] Can I do nothing for you?

BLENKINSOP. Well, if you have an old frock-coat to spare? you see what would be an old one for you would be

109

a new one for me; so remember the next time you turn out your wardrobe. Good-bye. [*He hurries out*].

RIDGEON [*looking after him*] Poor chap! [*Turning to Sir Patrick*] So thats why they made me a knight! And thats the medical profession!

SIR PATRICK. And a very good profession, to, my lad. When you know as much as I know of the ignorance and superstition of the patients, youll wonder that we're half as good as we are.

RIDGEON. We're not a profession: we're a conspiracy.

SIR PATRICK. All professions are conspiracies against the laity. And we cant all be geniuses like you. Every fool can get ill; but every fool cant be a good dotor: there are not enough good ones to go round. And for all you know, Bloomfield Bonington kills less people than you do.

RIDGEON. Oh, very likely. But he really ought to know the difference between a vaccine and an anti-toxin. Stimulate the phagocytes! The vaccine doesnt affect the phagocytes at all. He's all wrong: hopelessly, dangerously wrong. To put a tube of serum into his hands is murder: simple murder.

EMMY [*returning*] Now, Sir Patrick. How long more are you going to keep them horses standing in the draught?

SIR PATRICK. Whats that to you, you old catamaran?

EMMY. Come, come, now! none of your temper to me. And it's time for Colly to get to his work.

RIDGEON. Behave yourself, Emmy. Get out.

EMMY. Oh, I learnt how to behave myself before I learnt you to do it. I know what doctors are: sitting talking together about themselves when they ought to be with their poor patients. And I know what horses are, Sir Patrick. I was brought up in the country. Now be good; and come along.

SIR PATRICK [*rising*] Very well, very well, very well. Good-bye, Colly. [*He pats Ridgeon on the shoulder and goes out, turning for a moment at the door to look meditatively at Emmy and say, with grave conviction*] You *a r e*

110

THE DOCTOR'S DILEMMA

an ugly old devil, and no mistake.

EMMY [*highly indignant, calling after him*] Youre no beauty yourself. [*To Ridgeon, much flustered*] Theyve no manners: they think they can say what they like to me; and you set them on, you do. I'll teach them their places. Here now: are you going to see that poor thing or are you not?

RIDGEON. I tell you for the fiftieth time I wont see anybody. Send her away.

EMMY. Oh, I'm tired of being told to send her away. What good will that do her?

RIDGEON. Must I get angry with you, Emmy?

EMMY [*coaxing*] Come now: just see her for a minute to please me: theres a good boy. She's given me half-a-crown. She thinks it's life and death to her husband for her to see you.

RIDGEON. Values her husband's life at half-a-crown!

EMMY. Well, it's all she can afford, poor lamb. Them others think nothing of half-a-sovereign just to talk about themselves to you, the sluts! Besides, she'll put you in a good temper for the day, because it's a good deed to see her; and she's the sort that gets round you.

RIDGEON. Well, she hasnt done so badly. For half-a-crown she's had a consultation with Sir Ralph Bloomfield Bonington and Cutler Walpole. Thats six guineas' worth to start with. I dare say she's consulted Blenkinsop too: thats another eighteenpence.

EMMY. Then youll see her for me, wont you?

RIDGEON. Oh, send her up and be hanged. [*Emmy trots out, satisfied. Ridgeon calls*] Redpenny!

REDPENNY [*appearing at the door*] What is it?

RIDGEON. Theres a patient coming up. If she hasnt gone in five minutes, come in with an urgent call from the hospital for me. You understand: she's to have a strong hint to go.

REDPENNY. Right O! [*He vanishes*].

Ridgeon goes to the glass, and arranges his tie a little.

EMMY [*announcing*] Mrs Doobidad. [*Ridgeon leaves*

111

the glass and goes to the writing-table].

The lady comes in. Emmy goes out and shuts the door. Ridgeon, who has put on an impenetrable and rather distant professional manner, turns to the lady, and invites her, by a gesture, to sit down on the couch.

Mrs. Dubedat is beyond all demur an arrestingly good-looking young woman. She has something of the grace and romance of a mild creature, with a good deal of the elegance and dignity of a fine lady. Ridgeon, who is extremely susceptible to the beauty of women, instinctively assumes the defensive at once, and hardens his manner still more. He has an impression that she is very well dressed; but she has a figure on which any dress would look well, and carries herself with the unaffected distinction of a woman who has never in her life suffered from those doubts and fears as to her social position which spoil the manners of most middling people. She is tall, slender, and strong; has dark hair, dressed so as to look like hair and not like a bird's nest or a pantaloon's wig (fashion wavering just then between these two models); has unexpectedly narrow, subtle, dark-fringed eyes that alter her expression disturbingly when she is excited and flashes them wide open; is softly impetuous in her speech and swift in her movements; and is just now in mortal anxiety. She carries a portfolio.

MRS DUBEDAT [*in low urgent tones*] Doctor—

RIDGEON [*curtly*] Wait. Before you begin, let me tell you at once that I can do nothing for you. My hands are full. I sent you that message by my old servant. You would not take that answer.

MRS DUBEDAT. How could I?

RIDGEON. You bribed her.

MRS DUBEDAT. I—

RIDGEON. That doesnt matter. She coaxed me to see you. Well, you must take it from me now that with all the good will in the world, I cannot undertake another case.

MRS DUBEDAT. Doctor: you must save my husband. You must. When I explain to you, you will see that you

112

must. It is not an ordinary case, not like any other case. He is not like anybody else in the world: oh, believe me, he is not. I can prove it to you: [*fingering her portfolio*] I have brought some things to shew you. And you can save him: the papers say you can.

RIDGEON. Whats the matter? Tuberculosis?

MRS DUBEDAT. Yes. His left lung—

RIDGEON. Yes: you neednt tell me about that.

MRS DUBEDAT. You c a n cure him, if only you will. It is true that you can, isnt it? [*In great distress*] Oh, tell me, please.

RIDGEON [*warningly*] You are going to be quiet and self-possessed, arnt you?

MRS. DUBEDAT. Yes. I beg your pardon. I know I shouldnt—[*Giving way again*] Oh, please, say that you c a n; and then I shall be all right.

RIDGEON [*huffily*] I am not a curemonger: if you want cures, you must go to the people who sell them. [*Recovering himself, ashamed of the tone of his own voice*] But I have at the hospital ten tuberculous patients whose lives I believe I can save.

MRS DUBEDAT. Thank God!

RIDGEON. Wait a moment. Try to think of those ten patients as ten shipwrecked men on a raft—a raft that is barely large enough to save them—that will not support one more. Another head bobs up through the waves at the side. Another man begs to be taken aboard. He implores the captain of the raft to save him. But the captain can only do that by pushing one of his ten off the raft and drowning him to make room for the new comer. That is what you are asking me to do.

MRS DUBEDAT. But how can that be? I dont understand. Surely—

RIDGEON. You must take my word for it that it is so. My laboratory, my staff, and myself are working at full pressure. We are doing our utmost. The treatment is a new one. It takes time, means, and skill; and there is not enough

THE DOCTOR'S DILEMMA

for another case. Our ten cases are already chosen cases. Do you understand what I mean by chosen?

MRS DUBEDAT. Chosen. No: I cant understand.

RIDGEON [*sternly*] You m u s t understand. Youve got to understand and to face it. In every single one of those ten cases I have had to consider, not only whether the man could be saved, but whether he was worth saving. There were fifty cases to choose from; and forty had to be condemned to death. Some of the forty had young wives and helpless children. If the hardness of their cases could have saved them they would have been saved ten times over. Ive no doubt your case is a hard one: I can see the tears in your eyes [*she hastily wipes her eyes*]: I know that you have a torrent of entreaties ready for me the moment I stop speaking; but it's no use. You must go to another doctor.

MRS DUBEDAT. But can you give me the name of another doctor who understands your secret?

RIDGEON. I have no secret: I am not a quack.

MRS DUBEDAT. I beg your pardon: I didnt mean to say anything wrong. I dont understand how to speak to you. Oh, pray dont be offended.

RIDGEON [*again a little ashamed*] There! there! never mind. [*He relaxes and sits down*]. After all, I'm talking nonsense: I daresay I a m a quack, a quack with a qualification. But my discovery is not patented.

MRS DUBEDAT. Then can any doctor cure my husband? Oh, why dont they do it? I have tried so many: I have spent so much. If only you would give me the name of another doctor.

RIDGEON. Every man in this street is a doctor. But outside myself and the handful of men I am training at St Anne's, there is nobody as yet who has mastered the opsonin treatment. And we are f u l l up? I'm sorry; but that is all I can say. [*Rising*] Good morning.

MRS DUBEDAT [*suddenly and desperately taking some drawings from her portfolio*] Doctor: look at these. You understand drawings: you have good ones in your waiting-

114

room. Look at them. They are his work.

RIDGEON. It's no use my looking. [*He looks, all the same*] Hallo! [*He takes one to the window and studies it*]. Yes: this is the real thing. Yes, yes. [*He looks at another and returns to her*]. These are very clever. Theyre unfinished, arnt they?

MRS DUBEDAT. He gets tired so soon. But you see, dont you, what a genius he is? You see that he is worth saving. Oh, doctor, I married him just to help him to begin: I had money enough to tide him over the hard years at the beginning—to enable him to follow his inspiration until his genius was recognized. And I was useful to him as a model: his drawings of me sold quite quickly.

RIDGEON. Have you got one?

MRS DUBEDAT [*producing another*] Only this one. It was the first.

RIDGEON [*devouring it with his eyes*] Thats a wonderful drawing. Why is it called Jennifer?

MRS DUBEDAT. My name is Jennifer.

RIDGEON. A strange name.

MRS DUBEDAT. Not in Cornwall. I am Cornish. It's only what you call Guinevere.

RIDGEON [*repeating the names with a certain pleasure in them*] Guinevere. Jennifer. [*Looking again at the drawing*] Yes: it's really a wonderful drawing. Excuse me; but may I ask is it for sale? I'll buy it.

MRS DUBEDAT. Oh, take it. It's my own: he gave it to me. Take it. Take them all. Take everything; ask anything; but save him. You can: you will: you must.

REDPENNY [*entering with every sign of alarm*]. Theyve just telephoned from the hospital that youre to come instantly—a patient on the point of death. The carriage is waiting.

RIDGEON [*intolerantly*] Oh, nonsense: get out. [*Greatly annoyed*] What do you mean by interrupting me like this?

REDPENNY. But—

RIDGEON. Chut! cant you see I'm engaged? Be off.

THE DOCTOR'S DILEMMA

Redpenny, bewildered, vanishes.

MRS DUBEDAT [*rising*] Doctor: one instant only before you go—

RIDGEON. Sit down. It's nothing.

MRS DUBEDAT. But the patient. He said he was dying.

RIDGEON. Oh, he's dead by this time. Never mind. Sit down.

MRS DUBEDAT [*sitting down and breaking down*] Oh, you none of you care. You see people die every day.

RIDGEON [*petting her*] Nonsense! it's nothing: I told him to come in and say that. I thought I should want to get rid of you.

MRS DUBEDAT [*shocked at the falsehood*] Oh!

RIDGEON [*continuing*] Dont look so bewildered: theres nobody dying.

MRS DUBEDAT. My husband is.

RIDGEON [*pulling himself together*] Ah, yes: I had forgotten your husband. Mrs Dubedat: you are asking me to do a very serious thing?

MRS DUBEDAT. I am asking you to save the life of a great man.

RIDGEON. You are asking me to kill another man for his sake; for as surely as I undertake another case, I shall have to hand back one of the old ones to the ordinary treatment. Well, I dont shrink from that. I have had to do it before; and I will do it again if you can convince me that his life is more important than the worst life I am now saving. But you must convince me first.

MRS DUBEDAT. He made those drawings; and they are not the best—nothing like the best; only I did not bring the really best: so few people like them. He is twenty-three: his whole life is before him. Wont you let me bring him to you? wont you speak to him? wont you see for yourself?

RIDGEON. Is he well enough to come to a dinner at the Star and Garter at Richmond?

116

THE DOCTOR'S DILEMMA

MRS DUBEDAT. Oh yes. Why?

RIDGEON. I'll tell you. I am inviting all my old friends to a dinner to celebrate my knighthood—youve seen about it in the papers, havnt you?

MRS DUBEDAT. Yes, oh yes. That was how I found out about you.

RIDGEON. It will be a doctors' dinner; and it was to have been a bachelors' dinner. I'm a bachelor. Now if you will entertain for me, and bring your husband, he will meet me; and he will meet some of the most eminent men in my profession: Sir Patrick Cullen, Sir Ralph Bloomfield Bonington, Cutler Walpole, and others. I can put the case to them; and your husband will have to stand or fall by what we think of him. Will you come?

MRS DUBEDAT. Yes, of course I will come. Oh, thank you, thank you. And may I bring some of his drawings—the really good ones?

RIDGEON. Yes. I will let you know the date in the course of to-morrow. Leave me your address.

MRS DUBEDAT. Thank you again and again. You have made me so happy: I know you will admire him and like him. This is my address. [*She gives him her card*].

RIDGEON. Thank you. [*He rings*].

MRS DUBEDAT [*embarrassed*] May I—is there—should I—I mean—[*she blushes and stops in confusion*].

RIDGEON. Whats the matter?

MRS DUBEDAT. Your fee for this consultation?

RIDGEON. Oh, I forgot that. Shall we say a beautiful drawing of his favorite model for the whole treatment, including the cure?

MRS DUBEDAT. You are very generous. Thank you. I know you will cure him. Good-bye.

RIDGEON. I will. Good-bye. [*They shake hands*]. By the way, you know, dont you, that tuberculosis is catching. You take every precaution, I hope.

MRS DUBEDAT. I am not likely to forget it. They treat us

117

like lepers at the hotels.

EMMY [*at the door*] Well, deary: have you got round him?

RIDGEON. Yes. Attend to the door and hold your tongue.

EMMY. Thats a good boy. [*She goes out with Mrs Dubedat*].

RIDGEON [*alone*] Consultation free. Cure guaranteed. [*He heaves a great sigh*].

ACT II

AFTER *dinner on the terrace at the Star and Garter, Richmond. Cloudless summer night; nothing disturbs the stillness except from time to time the long trajectory of a distant train and the measured clucking of oars coming up from the Thames in the valley below. The dinner is over; and three of the eight chairs are empty. Sir Patrick, with his back to the view, is at the head of the square table with Ridgeon. The two chairs opposite them are empty. On their right come, first, a vacant chair, and then one very fully occupied by B. B., who basks blissfully in the moonbeams. On their left, Schutzmacher and Walpole. The entrance to the hotel is on their right, behind B. B. The five men are silently enjoying their coffee and cigarets, full of food, and not altogether void of wine.*

Mrs Dubedat, wrapped up for departure, comes in. They rise, except Sir Patrick; but she takes one of the vacant places at the foot of the table, next B. B.; and they sit down again.

MRS DUBEDAT [*as she enters*] Louis will be here presently. He is shewing Dr Blenkinsop how to work the telephone. [*She sits.*] Oh, I am so sorry we have to go. It seems such a shame, this beautiful night. And we have enjoyed ourselves so much.

RIDGEON. I dont believe another half-hour would do Mr Dubedat a bit of harm.

SIR PATRICK. Come now, Colly, come! come! none of that. You take your man home, Mrs Dubedat; and get him to bed before eleven.

B. B. Yes, yes. Bed before eleven. Quite right, quite right. Sorry to lose you, my dear lady; but Sir Patrick's orders are the laws of—er—of Tyre and Sidon.

WALPOLE. Let me take you home in my motor.

SIR PATRICK. No. You ought to be ashamed of yourself, Walpole. Your motor will take Mr and Mrs Dubedat to

119

the station, and quite far enough too for an open carriage at night.

MRS DUBEDAT. Oh, I am sure the train is best.

RIDGEON. Well, Mrs Dubedat, we have had a most enjoyable evening.

WALPOLE. { Most enjoyable.

B. B. { Delightful. Charming. Unforgettable.

MRS DUBEDAT [*with a touch of shy anxiety*] What did you think of Louis? Or am I wrong to ask?

RIDGEON. Wrong! Why, we are all charmed with him.

WALPOLE. Delighted.

B. B. Most happy to have met him. A privilege, a real privilege.

SIR PATRICK [*grunts*]!

MRS DUBEDAT [*quickly*] Sir Patrick: are y o u uneasy about him?

SIR PATRICK [*discreetly*] I admire his drawings greatly, maam.

MRS DUBEDAT. Yes; but I meant—

RIDGEON. You shall go away quite happy. He's worth saving. He must and shall be saved.

Mrs Dubedat rises and gasps with delight, relief, and gratitude. They all rise except Sir Patrick and Schutzmacher, and come reassuringly to her.

B. B. Certainly, c e r-tainly.

WALPOLE. Theres no real difficulty, if only you know what to do.

MRS DUBEDAT. Oh, how can I ever thank you! From this night I can begin to be happy at last. You dont know what I feel.

She sits down in tears. They crowd about her to console her.

B. B. My dear lady: come come! come come! [*very persuasively*] c o m e come!

WALPOLE. Dont mind us. Have a good cry.

RIDGEON. No: dont cry. Your husband had better not

know that weve been talking about him.

MRS DUBEDAT [*quickly pulling herself together*] No, of course not. Please dont mind me. What a glorious thing it must be to be a doctor! [*They laugh*]. Dont laugh. You dont know what youve done for me. I never knew until now how deadly afraid I was—how I had come to dread the worst. I never dared let myself know. But now the relief has come: now I know.

Louis Dubedat comes from the hotel, in his overcoat, his throat wrapped in a shawl. He is a slim young man of 23, physically still a stripling, and pretty, though not effeminate. He has turquoise blue eyes, and a trick of looking you straight in the face with them, which, combined with a frank smile, is very engaging. Although he is all nerves, and very observant and quick of apprehension, he is not in the least shy. He is younger than Jennifer; but he patronizes her as a matter of course. The doctors do not put him out in the least: neither Sir Patrick's years nor Bloomfield Bonington's majesty have the smallest apparent effect on him: he is as natural as a cat: he moves among men as most men move among things, though he is intentionally making himself agreeable to them on this occasion. Like all people who can be depended on to take care of themselves, he is welcome company; and his artist's power of appealing to the imagination gains him credit for all sorts of qualities and powers, whether he possesses them or not.

LOUIS [*pulling on his gloves behind Ridgeon's chair*] Now, Jinny-Gwinny: the motor has come round.

RIDGEON. Why do you let him spoil your beautiful name like that, Mrs Dubedat?

MRS DUBEDAT. Oh, on grand occasions I am Jennifer.

B. B. You are a bachelor: you do not understand these things, Ridgeon. Look at me [*They look*]. I also have two names. In moments of domestic worry, I am simple Ralph. When the sun shines in the home, I am Beedle-Deedle-Dumkins. Such is married life! Mr Dubedat: may I ask you to do me a favor before you go. Will you sign your name to this menu card, under the sketch you have made of me?

WALPOLE. Yes; and mine too, if you will be so good.

LOUIS. Certainly. [*He sits down and signs the cards*].

MRS DUBEDAT. Wont you sign Dr Schutzmacher's for him, Louis?

LOUIS. I dont think Dr Schutzmacher is pleased with his portrait. I'll tear it up. [*He reaches across the table for Schutzmacher's menu card, and is about to tear it. Schutzmacher makes no sign*].

RIDGEON. No, no: if Loony doesnt want it, I do.

LOUIS. I'll sign it for you with pleasure. [*He signs and hands it to Ridgeon*]. Ive just been making a little note of the river to-night: it will work up into something good [*he shews a pocket sketch-book*]. I think I'll call it the Silver Danube.

B. B. Ah, charming, charming.

WALPOLE. Very sweet. Youre a nailer at pastel.

Louis coughs, first out of modesty, then from tuberculosis.

SIR PATRICK. Now then, Mr Dubedat: youve had enough of the night air. Take him home, maam.

MRS DUBEDAT. Yes. Come, Louis.

RIDGEON. Never fear. Never mind. I'll make that cough all right.

B. B. We will stimulate the phagocytes. [*With tender effusion, shaking her hand*] G o o d-night, Mrs Dubedat. Good-night. Good-night.

WALPOLE. If the phagocytes fail, come to me. I'll put you right.

LOUIS. Good-night, Sir Patrick. Happy to have met you.

SIR PATRICK. 'Night [*half a grunt*].

MRS DUBEDAT. Good-night, Sir Patrick.

SIR PATRICK. Cover yourself well up. Dont think your

lungs are made of iron because theyre better than his. Good-night.

MRS DUBEDAT. Thank you. Thank you. Nothing hurts me. Good-night.

Louis goes out through the hotel without noticing Schutzmacher. Mrs Dubedat hesitates, then bows to him. Schutzmacher rises and bows formally, German fashion. She goes out, attended by Ridgeon. The rest resume their seats, ruminating or smoking quietly.

B. B. [*harmoniously*] Dee-lightful couple! Charming woman! Gifted lad! Remarkable talent! Graceful out-lines! Perfect evening! Great success! Interesting case! Glorious night! Exquisite scenery! Capital dinner! Stimulating conversation! Restful outing! Good wine! Happy ending! Touching gratitude! Lucky Ridgeon—

RIDGEON [*returning*] Whats that? Calling me, B. B.? [*He goes back to his seat next Sir Patrick*].

B. B. No, no. Only congratulating you on a most success-ful evening! Enchanting woman! Thorough breeding! Gentle nature! Refined—

Blenkinsop comes from the hotel and takes the empty chair next Ridgeon.

BLENKINSOP. I'm so sorry to have left you like this, Ridgeon; but it was a telephone message from the police. Theyve found half a milkman at our level crossing with a prescription of mine in its pocket. Wheres Mr Dubedat?

RIDGEON. Gone.

BLENKINSOP [*rising, very pale*] Gone!

RIDGEON. Just this moment—

BLENKINSOP. Perhaps I could overtake him—[*he rushes into the hotel*].

WALPOLE [*calling after him*] He's in the motor, man, miles off. You can—[*giving it up*]. No use.

RIDGEON. Theyre really very nice people. I confess I was afraid the husband would turn out an appalling bounder. But he's almost as charming in his way as she is in

123

hers. And theres no mistake about his being a genius. It's something to have got a case really worth saving. Somebody else will have to go; but at all events it will be easy to find a worse man.

SIR PATRICK. How do you know?

RIDGEON. Come now, Sir Paddy, no growling. Have something more to drink.

SIR PATRICK. No, thank you.

WALPOLE. Do y o u see anything wrong with Dubedat, B. B.?

B. B. Oh, a charming young fellow. Besides, after all, what c o u l d be wrong with him? L o o k at him. What c o u l d be wrong with him?

SIR PATRICK. There are two things that can be wrong with any man. One of them is a cheque. The other is a woman. Until you know that a man's sound on these two points, you know nothing about him.

B. B. Ah, cynic, cynic!

WALPOLE. He's all right as to the cheque, for a while at all events. He talked to me quite frankly before dinner as to the pressure of money difficulties on an artist. He says he has no vices and is very economical, but that theres one extravagance he cant afford and yet cant resist; and that is dressing his wife prettily. So I said, bang plump out, "Let me lend you twenty pounds, and pay me when your ship comes home." He was really very nice about it. He took it like a man; and it was a pleasure to see how happy it made him, poor chap.

B. B. [*who has listened to Walpole with growing perturbation*] But—but—but—when was this, may I ask?

WALPOLE. When I joined you that time down by the river.

B. B. But, my dear Walpole, he had just borrowed ten pounds from me.

WALPOLE. What!

SIR PATRICK [*grunts*]!

124

B. B. [*indulgently*] Well, well, it was really hardly borrowing; for he said heaven only knew when he could pay me. I couldnt refuse. It appears that Mrs Dubedat has taken a sort of fancy to me—

WALPOLE [*quickly*] No: it was to me.

B. B. Certainly not. Your name was never mentioned between us. He is so wrapped up in his work that he has to leave her a good deal alone; and the poor innocent young fellow—he has of course no idea of my position or how busy I am—actually wanted me to call occasionally and talk to her.

WALPOLE. Exactly what he said to me!

B. B. Pooh! Pooh pooh! Really, I must say. [*Much disturbed, he rises and goes up to the balustrade, contemplating the landscape vexedly*].

WALPOLE. Look here, Ridgeon! this is beginning to look serious.

Blenkinsop, very anxious and wretched, but trying to look unconcerned, comes back.

RIDGEON. Well, did you catch him?

BLENKINSOP. No. Excuse my running away like that. [*He sits down at the foot of the table, next Bloomfield Bonington's chair*].

WALPOLE. Anything the matter?

BLENKINSOP. Oh no. A trifle—something ridiculous. It cant be helped. Never mind.

RIDGEON. Was it anything about Dubedat?

BLENKINSOP [*almost breaking down*] I ought to keep it to myself, I know. I cant tell you, Ridgeon, how ashamed I am of dragging my miserable poverty to your dinner after all your kindness. It's not that you wont ask me again; but it's so humiliating. And I did so look forward to one evening in my dress clothes (t h e y r e still presentable, you see) with all my troubles left behind, just like old times.

RIDGEON. But what has happened?

BLENKINSOP. Oh, nothing. It's too ridiculous. I had just scraped up four shillings for this little outing; and it

THE DOCTOR'S DILEMMA

cost me one-and-fourpence to get here. Well, Dubedat asked me to lend him half-a-crown to tip the chambermaid of the room his wife left her wraps in, and for the cloakroom. He said he only wanted it for five minutes, as she had his purse. So of course I lent it to him. And he's forgotten to pay me. I've just tuppence to get back with.

RIDGEON. Oh, never mind that—

BLENKINSOP [*stopping him resolutely*] No: I know what youre going to say; but I wont take it. Ive never borrowed a penny; and I never will. Ive nothing left but my friends; and I wont sell them. If none of you were to be able to meet me without being afraid that my civility was leading up to the loan of five shillings, there would be an end of everything for me. I'll take your old clothes, Colly, sooner than disgrace you by talking to you in the street in my own; but I wont borrow money. I'll train it as far as the twopence will take me; and I'll tramp the rest.

WALPOLE. Youll do the whole distance in my motor. [*They are all greatly relieved; and Walpole hastens to get away from the painful subject by adding*] Did he get anything out of y o u, Mr Schutzmacher?

SCHUTZMACHER [*shakes his head in a most expressive negative*].

WALPOLE. You didnt appreciate his drawing, I think.

SCHUTZMACHER. Oh yes I did. I should have liked very much to have kept the sketch and got it autographed.

B. B. But why didnt you?

SCHUTZMACHER. Well, the fact is, when I joined Dubedat after his conversation with Mr Walpole, he said the Jews were the only people who knew anything about art, and that though he had to put up with your Philistine twaddle, as he called it, it was what I said about the drawings that really pleased him. He also said that his wife was greatly struck with my knowledge, and that she always admired Jews. Then he asked me to advance him £50 on the security of the drawings.

126

THE DOCTOR'S DILEMMA

B. B.		No, no. Positively! Seriously!
WALPOLE	*[All exclaiming together]*	What! Another fifty!
BLENKINSOP		Think of that!
SIR PATRICK		*[grunts]*!

SCHUTZMACHER. Of course I couldnt lend money to a stranger like that.

B. B. I envy you the power to say No, Mr Schutzmacher. Of course, I knew I oughtnt to lend money to a young fellow in that way; but I simply hadnt the nerve to refuse. I couldnt very well, you know, could I?

SCHUTZMACHER. I dont understand that. *I* felt that I couldnt very well lend it.

WALPOLE. What did he say?

SCHUTZMACHER. Well, he made a very uncalled-for remark about a Jew not understanding the feelings of a gentleman. I must say you Gentiles are very hard to please. You say we are no gentlemen when we lend money; and when we refuse to lend it you say just the same. I didnt mean to behave badly. As I told him, I might have lent it to him if he had been a Jew himself.

SIR PATRICK *[with a grunt]*. And what did he say to that?

SCHUTZMACHER. Oh, he began trying to persuade me that he was one of the chosen people—that his artistic faculty shewed it, and that his name was as foreign as my own. He said he didnt really want £50; that he was only joking; that all he wanted was a couple of sovereigns.

B. B. No, no, Mr Schutzmacher. You invented that last touch. Seriously, now?

SCHUTZMACHER. No. You cant improve on Nature in telling stories about gentlemen like Mr Dubedat.

BLENKINSOP. You certainly do stand by one another, you chosen people, Mr Schutzmacher.

SCHUTZMACHER. Not at all. Personally, I like Englishmen better than Jews, and always associate with them.

127

Thats only natural, because, as I am a Jew, theres nothing interesting in a Jew to me, whereas there is always something interesting and foreign in an Englishman. But in money matters it's quite different. You see, when an Englishman borrows, all he knows or cares is that he wants money; and he'll sign anything to get it, without in the least understanding it, or intending to carry out the agreement if it turns out badly for him. In fact, he thinks you a cad if you ask him to carry it out under such circumstances. Just like the Merchant of Venice, you know. But if a Jew makes an agreement, he means to keep it and expects you to keep it. If he wants money for a time, he borrows it and knows he must pay it at the end of the time. If he knows he cant pay, he begs it as a gift.

RIDGEON. Come, Loony! do you mean to say that Jews are never rogues and thieves?

SCHUTZMACHER. Oh, not at all. But I was not talking of criminals. I was comparing honest Englishmen with honest Jews.

One of the hotel maids, a pretty, fair-haired woman of about 25, comes from the hotel, rather furtively. She accosts Ridgeon.

THE MAID. I beg your pardon, sir—

RIDGEON. Eh?

THE MAID. I beg pardon, sir. It's not about the hotel. I'm not allowed to be on the terrace; and I should be discharged if I were seen speaking to you, unless you were kind enough to say you called me to ask whether the motor has come back from the station yet.

WALPOLE. Has it?

THE MAID. Yes, sir.

RIDGEON. Well, what do you want?

THE MAID. Would you mind, sir, giving me the address of the gentleman that was with you at dinner?

RIDGEON [*sharply*] Yes, of course I should mind very much. You have no right to ask.

128

THE MAID. Yes, sir, I know it looks like that. But what am I to do?

SIR PATRICK. Whats the matter with you?

THE MAID. Nothing, sir. I want the address: thats all.

B. B. You mean the young gentleman?

THE MAID. Yes, sir: that went to catch the train with the woman he brought with him.

RIDGEON. The woman! Do you mean the l a d y who dined here? the gentleman's wife?

THE MAID. Dont believe them, sir. She cant be his wife. I'm his wife.

B. B. [*in amazed remonstrance*] My good girl!

RIDGEON You his wife!

WALPOLE What! whats that? Oh, this is getting perfectly fascinating, Ridgeon.

THE MAID. I could run upstairs and get you my marriage lines in a minute, sir, if you doubt my word. He's Mr Louis Dubedat, isnt he?

RIDGEON. Yes.

THE MAID. Well, sir, you may believe me or not; but I'm the lawful Mrs Dubedat.

SIR PATRICK. And why arnt you living with your husband?

THE MAID. We couldnt afford it, sir. I had thirty pounds saved; and we spent it all on our honeymoon in three weeks, and a lot more that he borrowed. Then I had to go back into service, and he went to London to get work at his drawing; and he never wrote me a line or sent me an address. I never saw nor heard of him again until I caught sight of him from the window going off in the motor with that woman.

SIR PATRICK. Well, thats two wives to start with.

B. B. Now upon my soul I dont want to be uncharitable; but really I'm beginning to suspect that our young friend is rather careless.

129

SIR PATRICK. Beginning to think! How long will it take you, man, to find out that he's a damned young blackguard?

BLENKINSOP. Oh, thats severe, Sir Patrick, very severe. Of course it's bigamy; but still he's very young; and she's very pretty. Mr Walpole: may I spunge on you for another of those nice cigarets of yours? [*He changes his seat for the one next Walpole*].

WALPOLE. Certainly. [*He feels in his pockets*]. Oh bother! Where—? [*Suddenly remembering*] I say: I recollect now: I passed my cigaret case to Dubedat and he didnt return it. It was a gold one.

THE MAID. He didnt mean any harm: he never thinks about things like that, sir. I'll get it back for you, sir, if youll tell me where to find him.

RIDGEON. What am I to do? Shall I give her the address or not?

SIR PATRICK. Give her your own address; and then we'll see. [*To the maid*] Youll have to be content with that for the present, my girl. [*Ridgeon gives her his card*]. Whats your name?

THE MAID. Minnie Tinwell, sir.

SIR PATRICK. Well, you write him a letter to care of this gentleman; and it will be sent on. Now be off with you.

THE MAID. Thank you, sir. I'm sure you wouldnt see me wronged. Thank you all, gentlemen; and excuse the liberty.

She goes into the hotel. They watch her in silence.

RIDGEON [*when she is gone*] Do you realize, you chaps, that we have promised Mrs Dubedat to save this fellow's life?

BLENKINSOP. Whats the matter with him?

RIDGEON. Tuberculosis.

BLENKINSOP [*interested*] And can you cure that?

RIDGEON. I believe so.

BLENKINSOP. Then I wish youd cure me. My right lung is touched, I'm sorry to say.

THE DOCTOR'S DILEMMA

RIDGEON ⎫

          ⎪

B. B. ⎪

          ⎬ *[all together]*

          ⎪

SIR PATRICK ⎪

WALPOLE ⎭

What! y o u r lung is going!

My dear Blenkinsop, what do you tell me? *[full of concern for Blenkinsop, he comes back from the balustrade]*.

Eh? Eh? whats that?

Hullo! you mustnt neglect this, you know.

BLENKINSOP *[putting his fingers in his ears]* No, no: it's no use. I know what youre going to say: Ive said it often to others. I cant afford to take care of myself; and theres an end of it. If a fortnight's holiday would save my life, I'd have to die. I shall get on as others have to get on. We cant all go to St Moritz or to Egypt, you know, Sir Ralph. Dont talk about it.

Embarrassed silence.

SIR PATRICK *[grunts and looks hard at Ridgeon]*!

SCHUTZMACHER *[looking at his watch and rising]* I must go. It's been a very pleasant evening, Colly. You might let me have my portrait if you dont mind. I'll send Mr Dubedat that couple of sovereigns for it.

RIDGEON *[giving him the menu card]* Oh dont do that, Loony. I dont think he'd like that.

SCHUTZMACHER. Well, of course I shant if you feel that way about it. But I dont think you understand Dubedat. However, perhaps thats because I'm a Jew. Good-night, Dr Blenkinsop *[shaking hands]*.

BLENKINSOP. Good-night, sir—I mean—Good-night.

SCHUTZMACHER *[waving his hand to the rest]* Good-night, everybody.

WALPOLE ⎫

B. B. ⎪

          ⎬ Good-night.

SIR PATRICK ⎪

RIDGEON ⎭

131

THE DOCTOR'S DILEMMA

B. B. repeats the salutation several times, in varied musical tones. Schutzmacher goes out.

SIR PATRICK. It's time for us all to move. [*He rises and comes between Blenkinsop and Walpole. Ridgeon also rises*]. Mr. Walpole: take Blenkinsop home: he's had enough of the open air cure for to-night. Have you a thick overcoat to wear in the motor, Dr Blenkinsop?

BLENKINSOP. Oh, theyll give me some brown paper in the hotel; and a few thicknesses of brown paper across the chest are better than any fur coat.

WALPOLE. Well, come along. Good-night, Colly. Youre coming with us, arnt you, B. B.?

B. B. Yes: I'm coming. [*Walpole and Blenkinsop go into the hotel*]. Good-night, my dear Ridgeon [*shaking hands affectionately*]. Dont let us lose sight of your interesting patient and his very charming wife. We must not judge him too hastily, you know. [*With unction*] G o o o o o o o o d-night, Paddy. Bless you, dear old chap. [*Sir Patrick utters a formidable grunt. B. B. laughs and pats him indulgently on the shoulder*] Good-night. Good-night. Good-night. Good-night. [*He good-nights himself into the hotel*].

The others have meanwhile gone without ceremony. Ridgeon and Sir Patrick are left alone together. Ridgeon, deep in thought, comes down to Sir Patrick.

SIR PATRICK. Well, Mr Savior of Lives: which is it to be? that honest decent man Blenkinsop, or that rotten blackguard of an artist, eh?

RIDGEON. It's not an easy case to judge, is it? Blenkinsop's an honest decent man; but is he any use? Dubedat's a rotten blackguard; but he's a genuine source of pretty and pleasant and good things.

SIR PATRICK. What will he be a source of for that poor innocent wife of his, when she finds him out?

RIDGEON. Thats true. Her life will be a hell.

SIR PATRICK. And tell me this. Suppose you had this choice put before you: either to go through life and find all

132

the pictures bad but all the men and women good, or to go through life and find all the pictures good and all the men and women rotten. Which would you choose?

RIDGEON. Thats a devilishly difficult question, Paddy. The pictures are so agreeable, and the good people so infernally disagreeable and mischievous, that I really cant undertake to say offhand which I should prefer to do without.

SIR PATRICK. Come come! none of your cleverness with me: I'm too old for it. Blenkinsop isnt that sort of good man; and you know it.

RIDGEON. It would be simpler if Blenkinsop could paint Dubedat's pictures.

SIR PATRICK. It would be simpler still if Dubedat had some of Blenkinsop's honesty. The world isnt going to be made simple for you, my lad: you must take it as it is. Youve to hold the scales between Blenkinsop and Dubedat. Hold them fairly.

RIDGEON. Well, I'll be as fair as I can. I'll put into one scale all the pounds Dubedat has borrowed, and into the other all the half-crowns that Blenkinsop hasnt borrowed.

SIR PATRICK. And youll take out of Dubedat's scale all the faith he has destroyed and the honor he has lost, and youll put into Blenkinsop's scale all the faith he has justified and the honor he has created.

RIDGEON. Come come, Paddy! none of your claptrap with me: I'm too sceptical for it. I'm not at all convinced that the world wouldnt be a better world if everybody behaved as Dubedat does than it is now that everybody behaves as Blenkinsop does.

SIR PATRICK. Then why dont y o u behave as Dubedat does?

RIDGEON. Ah, that beats me. Thats the experimental test. Still, it's a dilemma. It's a dilemma. You see theres a complication we havnt mentioned.

SIR PATRICK. Whats that?

RIDGEON. Well, if I let Blenkinsop die, at least nobody

133

can say I did it because I wanted to marry his widow.

SIR PATRICK. Eh? Whats that?

RIDGEON. Now if I let Dubedat die, I'll marry his widow.

SIR PATRICK. Perhaps she wont have you, you know.

RIDGEON [*with a self-assured shake of the head*] Ive a pretty good flair for that sort of thing. I know when a woman is interested in me. She is.

SIR PATRICK. Well, sometimes a man knows best; and sometimes he knows worst. Youd much better cure them both.

RIDGEON. I cant. I'm at my limit. I can squeeze in one more case, but not two. I must choose.

SIR PATRICK. Well, you must choose as if she didn't exist: thats clear.

RIDGEON. Is that clear to you? Mind: it's not clear to me. She troubles my judgment.

SIR PATRICK. To me, it's a plain choice between a man and a lot of pictures.

RIDGEON. It's easier to replace a dead man than a good picture.

SIR PATRICK. Colly: when you live in an age that runs to pictures and statues and plays and brass bands because its men and women are not good enough to comfort its poor aching soul, you should thank Providence that you belong to a profession which is a high and great profession because its business is to heal and mend men and women.

RIDGEON. In short, as a member of a high and great profession, I'm to kill my patient.

SIR PATRICK. Dont talk wicked nonsense. You cant kill him. But you can leave him in other hands.

RIDGEON. In B. B.'s, for instance: eh? [*looking at him significantly*].

SIR PATRICK [*demurely facing his look*] Sir Ralph Bloomfield Bonington is a very eminent physician.

RIDGEON. He is.

SIR PATRICK. I'm going for my hat.

Ridgeon strikes the bell as Sir Patrick makes for the hotel. A waiter comes.

RIDGEON [*to the waiter*] My bill, please.

WAITER. Yes, sir.

He goes for it.

ACT III

IN Dubedat's studio. Viewed from the large window
the outer door is in the wall on the left at the near end.
The door leading to the inner rooms is in the opposite wall, at the far end. The facing wall has neither window nor door. The plaster on all the walls is uncovered
and undecorated, except by scrawlings of charcoal sketches
and memoranda. There is a studio throne (a chair on a dais)
a little to the left, opposite the inner door, and an easel to
the right, opposite the outer door, with a dilapidated chair at
it. Near the easel and against the wall is a bare wooden table
with bottles and jars of oil and medium, paint-smudged
rags, tubes of color, brushes, charcoal, a small lay figure, a
kettle and spirit-lamp, and other odds and ends. By the
table is a sofa, littered with drawing blocks, sketch-books,
loose sheets of paper, newspapers, books, and more smudged
rags. Next the outer door is an umbrella and hat stand,
occupied partly by Louis' hats and cloak and muffler, and
partly by odds and ends of costumes. There is an old piano
stool on the near side of this door. In the corner near the
inner door is a little tea-table. A lay figure, in a cardinal's
robe and hat, with an hour-glass in one hand and a scythe
slung on its back, smiles with inane malice at Louis, who,
in a milkman's smock much smudged with colors, is painting a piece of brocade which he has draped about his wife.
She is sitting on the throne, not interested in the painting,
and appealing to him very anxiously about another matter.

MRS DUBEDAT. Promise.

LOUIS [putting on a touch of paint with notable skill and
care and answering quite perfunctorily] I promise, my
darling.

MRS DUBEDAT. When you want money, you will always
come to me.

LOUIS. But it's so sordid, dearest. I hate money. I cant
keep always bothering you for money, money, money.
Thats what drives me sometimes to ask other people,

136

Mrs. Dubedat [*delighted*] "Ah, that's right."
Katharine Cornell and Bramwell Fletcher

though I hate doing it.

MRS DUBEDAT. It is far better to ask me, dear. It gives people a wrong idea of you.

LOUIS. But I want to spare your little fortune, and raise money on my own work. Dont be unhappy, love: I can easily earn enough to pay it all back. I shall have a one-man-show next season; and then there will be no more money troubles. [*Putting down his palette*] There! I mustnt do any more on that until it's bone-dry; so you may come down.

MRS DUBEDAT [*throwing off the drapery as she steps down, and revealing a plain frock of tussore silk*] But you have promised, remember, seriously and faithfully, never to borrow again until you have first asked me.

LOUIS. Seriously and faithfully. [*Embracing her*] Ah, my love, how right you are! how much it means to me to have you by me to guard me against living too much in the skies. On my solemn oath, from this moment forth I will never borrow another penny.

MRS DUBEDAT [*delighted*] Ah, thats right. Does his wicked worrying wife torment him and drag him down from the clouds. [*She kisses him*]. And now, dear, wont you finish those drawings for Maclean?

LOUIS. Oh, they dont matter. Ive got nearly all the money from him in advance.

MRS DUBEDAT. But, dearest, that is just the reason why you should finish them. He asked me the other day whether you really intended to finish them.

LOUIS. Confound his impudence! What the devil does he take me for? Now that just destroys all my interest in the beastly job. Ive a good mind to throw up the commission, and pay him back his money.

MRS DUBEDAT. We cant afford that, dear. You had better finish the drawings and have done with them. I think it is a mistake to accept money in advance.

LOUIS. But how are we to live?

MRS DUBEDAT. Well, Louis, it is getting hard enough

as it is, now that they are all refusing to pay except on delivery.

LOUIS. Damn those fellows! they think of nothing and care for nothing but their wretched money.

MRS DUBEDAT. Still, if they pay us, they ought to have what they pay for.

LOUIS [*coaxing*] There now: thats enough lecturing for to-day. Ive promised to be good, havnt I?

MRS DUBEDAT [*putting her arms round his neck*] You know that I hate lecturing, and that I dont for a moment misunderstand you, dear, dont you?

LOUIS [*fondly*] I know. I know. I'm a wretch; and youre an angel. Oh, if only I were strong enough to work steadily, I'd make my darling's house a temple, and her shrine a chapel more beautiful than was ever imagined. I cant pass the shops without wrestling with the temptation to go in and order all the really good things they have for you.

MRS DUBEDAT. I want nothing but you, dear. [*She gives him a caress, to which he responds so passionately that she disengages herself*]. There! be good now: remember that the doctors are coming this morning. Isnt it extraordinarily kind of them, Louis, to insist on coming? all of them, to consult about you?

LOUIS [*coolly*] Oh, I daresay they think it will be a feather in their cap to cure a rising artist. They wouldnt come if it didnt amuse them, anyhow. [*Someone knocks at the door*]. I say: it's not time yet, is it?

MRS DUDEBAT. No, not quite yet.

LOUIS [*opening the door and finding* RIDGEON *there*] Hello, Ridgeon. Delighted to see you. Come in.

MRS DUDEBAT [*shaking hands*] It's so good of you to come, doctor.

LOUIS. Excuse this place, wont you? It's only a studio, you know: theres no real convenience for living here. But we pig along somehow, thanks to Jennifer.

MRS DUBEDAT. Now I'll run away. Perhaps later on,

when youre finished with Louis, I may come in and hear the
verdict. [*Ridgeon bows rather constrainedly*]. Would you
rather I didnt?

RIDGEON. Not at all. Not at all.

*Mrs Dubedat looks at him, a little puzzled by his for-
mal manner; then goes into the inner room.*

LOUIS [*flippantly*] I say: dont look so grave. Theres
nothing awful going to happen, is there?

RIDGEON. No.

LOUIS. Thats all right. Poor Jennifer has been looking
forward to your visit more than you can imagine. Shes taken
quite a fancy to you, Ridgeon. The poor girl has nobody
to talk to: I'm always painting. [*Taking up a sketch*]
Theres a little sketch I made of her yesterday.

RIDGEON. She shewed it to me a fortnight ago when she
first called on me.

LOUIS [*quite unabashed*] Oh! did she? Good Lord!
how time does fly! I could have sworn I'd only just finished
it. It's hard for her here, seeing me piling up drawings and
nothing coming in for them. Of course I shall sell them
next year fast enough, after my one-man-show; but while
the grass grows the steed starves. I hate to have her coming to me for money, and having none to give her. But
what can I do?

RIDGEON. I understood that Mrs Dubedat had some
property of her own.

LOUIS. Oh yes, a little; but how could a man with any
decency of feeling touch that? Suppose I did, what would
she have to live on if I died? I'm not insured: cant afford the premiums. [*Picking out another drawing*] How do
you like that?

RIDGEON [*putting it aside*] I have not come here to-
day to look at your drawings. I have more serious and pressing business with you.

LOUIS. You want to sound my wretched lung. [*With
impulsive candor*] My dear Ridgeon: I'll be frank with
you. Whats the matter in this house isnt lungs but bills. It

doesnt matter about me; but Jennifer has actually to econ-omize in the matter of food. Youve made us feel that we can treat you as a friend. Will you lend us a hundred and fifty pounds?

RIDGEON. No.

LOUIS [*surprised*] Why not?

RIDGEON. I am not a rich man; and I want every penny I can spare and more for my researches.

LOUIS. You mean youd want the money back again.

RIDGEON. I presume people sometimes have that in view when they lend money.

LOUIS [*after a moment's reflection*] Well, I can man-age that for you. I'll give you a cheque—or see here: theres no reason why you shouldnt have your bit too: I'll give you a cheque for two hundred.

RIDGEON. Why not cash the cheque at once without troubling me?

LOUIS. Bless you! they wouldnt cash it: I'm overdrawn as it is. No: the way to work it is this. I'll post-date the cheque next October. In October Jennifer's dividends come in. Well, you present the cheque. It will be returned marked "refer to drawer" or some rubbish of that sort. Then you can take it to Jennifer, and hint that if the cheque isnt taken up at once I shall be put in prison. She'll pay you like a shot. Youll clear £50; and youll do me a real service; for I do want the money very badly, old chap, I assure you.

RIDGEON [*staring at him*] You see no objection to the transaction; and you anticipate none from me!

LOUIS. Well, what objection can there be? It's quite safe. I can convince you about the dividends.

RIDGEON. I mean on the score of its being—shall I say dishonorable?

LOUIS. Well, of course I shouldnt suggest it if I didnt want the money.

RIDGEON. Indeed! Well, you will have to find some other means of getting it.

LOUIS. Do you mean that you refuse?

140

THE DOCTOR'S DILEMMA

RIDGEON. Do I mean—! [*letting his indignation loose*] Of course I refuse, man. What do you take me for? How dare you make such a proposal to me?

Louis. Why not?

RIDGEON. Faugh! You would not understand me if I tried to explain. Now, once for all, I will not lend you a farthing. I should be glad to help your wife; but lending you money is no service to her.

LOUIS. Oh well, if youre in earnest about helping her, I'll tell you what you might do. You might get your patients to buy some of my things, or to give me a few portrait commissions.

RIDGEON. My patients call me in as a physician, not as a commercial traveller.

A knock at the door. Louis goes unconcernedly to open it, pursuing the subject as he goes.

LOUIS. But you must have great influence with them. You must know such lots of things about them—private things that they wouldnt like to have known. They wouldnt dare to refuse you.

RIDGEON [*exploding*] Well, upon my—

Louis opens the door, and admits Sir Patrick, Sir Ralph, and Walpole.

RIDGEON [*proceeding furiously*] Walpole: Ive been here hardly ten minutes; and already he's tried to borrow £150 from me. Then he proposed that I should get the money for him by blackmailing his wife; and youve just interrupted him in the act of suggesting that I should blackmail my patients into sitting to him for their portraits.

LOUIS. Well, Ridgeon, if this is what you call being an honorable man! I spoke to you in confidence.

SIR PATRICK. We're all going to speak to you in confidence, young man.

WALPOLE [*hanging his hat on the only peg left vacant on the hat-stand*] We shall make ourselves at home for half an hour, Dubedat. Dont be alarmed: youre a most fascinating chap; and we love you.

141

LOUIS. Oh, all right, all right. Sit down—anywhere you can. Take this chair, Sir Patrick [*indicating the one on the throne*]. Up-z-z-z! [*helping him up: Sir Patrick grunts and enthrones himself*]. Here you are, B. B. [*Sir Ralph glares at the familiarity; but Louis, quite undisturbed, puts a big book and a sofa cushion on the dais, on Sir Patrick's right; and B. B. sits down, under protest*]. Let me take your hat. [*He takes B. B.'s hat unceremoniously, and substitutes it for the cardinal's hat on the head of the lay figure, thereby ingeniously destroying the dignity of the conclave. He then draws the piano stool from the wall and offers it to Walpole*]. You dont mind this, Walpole, do you? [*Walpole accepts the stool, and puts his hand into his pocket for his cigaret case. Missing it, he is reminded of his loss*].

WALPOLE. By the way, I'll trouble you for my cigaret case, if you dont mind?

LOUIS. What cigaret case?

WALPOLE. The gold one I lent you at the Star and Garter.

LOUIS [*surprised*] Was that yours?

WALPOLE. Yes.

LOUIS. I'm awfully sorry, old chap. I wondered whose it was. I'm sorry to say this is all thats left of it. [*He hitches up his smock; produces a card from his waistcoat pocket; and hands it to Walpole*].

WALPOLE. A pawn ticket!

LOUIS [*reassuringly*] It's quite safe: he cant sell it for a year, you know. I say, my dear Walpole, I am sorry. [*He places his hand ingenuously on Walpole's shoulder and looks frankly at him*].

WALPOLE [*sinking on the stool with a gasp*] Dont mention it. It adds to your fascination.

RIDGEON [*who has been standing near the easel*] Before we go any further, you have a debt to pay, Mr Dubedat.

LOUIS. I have a precious lot of debts to pay, Ridgeon. I'll fetch you a chair. [*He makes for the inner door*].

RIDGEON [*stopping him*] You shall not leave the room

THE DOCTOR'S DILEMMA

until you pay it. It's a small one; and pay it you must and shall. I dont so much mind your borrowing £10 from one of my guests and £20 from the other—

WALPOLE. I walked into it, you know. I offered it.

RIDGEON. —they could afford it. But to clean poor Blenkinsop out of his last half-crown was damnable. I intend to give him that half-crown and to be in a position to pledge him my word that you paid it. I'll have that out of you, at all events.

B. B. Quite right, Ridgeon. Quite right. Come, young man! down with the dust. Pay up.

LOUIS. Oh, you neednt make such a fuss about it. Of course I'll pay it. I had no idea the poor fellow was hard up. I'm as shocked as any of you about it. [*Putting his hand into his pocket*] Here you are. [*Finding his pocket empty*] Oh, I say, I havnt any money on me just at present. Walpole: would you mind lending me half-a-crown just to settle this.

WALPOLE. Lend you half— [*his voice faints away*].

LOUIS. Well, if you dont, Blenkinsop wont get it; for I havnt a rap: you may search my pockets if you like.

WALPOLE. Thats conclusive. [*He produces half-a-crown*].

LOUIS [*passing it to Ridgeon*] There! I'm really glad thats settled: it was the only thing that was on my conscience. Now I hope youre all satisfied.

SIR PATRICK. Not quite, Mr Dubedat. Do you happen to know a young woman named Minnie Tinwell?

LOUIS. Minnie! I should think I do; and Minnie knows me too. She's a really nice good girl, considering her station. Whats become of her?

WALPOLE. It's no use b l u ffi n g, Dubedat. Weve seen Minnie's marriage lines.

LOUIS [*coolly*] Indeed? Have you seen Jennifer's?

RIDGEON [*rising in irrepressible rage*] Do you dare insinuate that Mrs Dubedat is living with you without being married to you?

143

THE DOCTOR'S DILEMMA

LOUIS. Why not?

B. B.	*[echoing him in*	Why not!
SIR PATRICK	*various tones of*	Why not!
RIDGEON	*scandalized*	Why not!
WALPOLE	*amazement]*	Why not!

LOUIS. Yes, why not? Lots of people do it: just as good people as you. Why dont you learn to think, instead of bleating and baahing like a lot of sheep when you come up against anything youre not accustomed to? [*Contemplating their amazed faces with a chuckle*] I say: I should like to draw the lot of you now: you do look jolly foolish. Especially you, Ridgeon. I had you that time, you know.

RIDGEON. How, pray?

LOUIS. Well, you set up to appreciate Jennifer, you know. And you despise me, dont you?

RIDGEON [*curtly*] I loathe you. [*He sits down again on the sofa*].

LOUIS. Just so. And yet you believe that Jennifer is a bad lot because you think I told you so.

RIDGEON. Were you lying?

LOUIS. No; but you were smelling out a scandal instead of keeping your mind clean and wholesome. I can just play with people like you. I only asked you had you seen Jennifer's marriage lines; and you concluded straight away that she hadnt got any. You dont know a lady when you see one.

. B. B. [*majestically*] What do you mean by that, may I ask?

LOUIS. Now, I'm only an immoral artist; but if youd told me that Jennifer wasnt married, I'd have had the gentlemanly feeling and artistic instinct to say that she carried her marriage certificate in her face and in her character. But y o u are all moral men; and Jennifer is only an artist's wife —probably a model; and morality consists in suspecting other people of not being legally married. Arnt you ashamed of yourselves? Can one of you look me in the face after it?

144

WALPOLE. It's very hard to look you in the face, Dubedat; you have such a dazzling cheek. What about Minnie Tinwell, eh?

LOUIS. Minnie Tinwell is a young woman who has had three weeks of glorious happiness in her poor little life, which is more than most girls in her position get, I can tell you. Ask her whether she'd take it back if she could. She's got her name into history, that girl. My little sketches of her will be bought by collectors at Christie's. She'll have a page in my biography. Pretty good, that, for a still-room maid at a seaside hotel, I think. What have you fellows done for her to compare with that?

RIDGEON. We havnt trapped her into a mock marriage and deserted her.

LOUIS. No: you wouldnt have the pluck. But dont fuss yourselves. *I* didnt desert little Minnie. We spent all our money—

WALPOLE. All h e r money. Thirty pounds.

LOUIS. I said all o u r money: hers and mine too. Her thirty pounds didnt last three days. I had to borrow four times as much to spend on her. But I didnt grudge it; and she didnt grudge her few pounds either, the brave little lassie. When we were cleaned out, we'd had enough of it: you can hardly suppose that we were fit company for longer than that: I an artist, and she quite out of art and literature and refined living and everything else. There was no desertion, no misunderstanding, no police court or divorce court sensation for you moral chaps to lick your lips over at breakfast. We just said, Well, the money's gone: weve had a good time that can never be taken from us; so kiss; part good friends; and she back to service, and I back to my studio and my Jennifer, both the better and happier for our holiday.

WALPOLE. Quite a little poem, by George!

. B. B. If you had been scientifically trained, Mr. Dubedat, you would know how very seldom an actual case bears out a principle. In medical practice a man may die when, scientifically speaking, he ought to have lived. I have actually known a man die of a disease from which he was scientifically speaking, immune. But that does not affect the fundamental truth of science. In just the same way, in moral cases, a man's behavior may be quite harmless and even beneficial, when he is morally behaving like a scoundrel. And he may do great harm when he is morally acting on the highest principles. But that does not affect the fundamental truth of morality.

SIR PATRICK. And it doesn't affect the criminal law on the subject of bigamy.

LOUIS. Oh bigamy! bigamy! bigamy! What a fascination anything connected with the police has for you all, you moralists! Ive proved to you that you were utterly wrong on the moral point: now I'm going to shew you that youre utterly wrong on the legal point; and I hope it will be a lesson to you not to be so jolly cocksure next time.

WALPOLE. Rot! You were married already when you married her; and that settles it.

LOUIS. Does it! Why cant you think? How do you know she wasnt married already too?

B. B.	*[all crying out together]*	Walpole! Ridgeon!
RIDGEON		This is beyond everything!
WALPOLE		Well, damn me!
SIR PATRICK		You young rascal.

LOUIS [*ignoring their outcry*] She was married to the steward of a liner. He cleared out and left her; and she thought, poor girl, that it was the law that if you hadnt heard of your husband for three years you might marry again. So as she was a thoroughly respectable girl and refused to have anything to say to me unless we were married I went through the ceremony to please her and to preserve her self-respect.

RIDGEON. Did you tell her you were already married?

LOUIS. Of course not. Dont you see that if she had known, she wouldnt have considered herself my wife? You

146

dont seem to understand, somehow.

SIR PATRICK. You let her risk imprisonment in her ignorance of the law?

LOUIS. Well, *I* risked imprisonment for her sake. I could have been had up for it just as much as she. But when a man makes a sacrifice of that sort for a woman, he doesnt go and brag about it to her; at least, not if he's a gentleman.

WALPOLE. What a r e we to do with this daisy?

LOUIS [*impatiently*] Oh, go and do whatever the devil you please. Put Minnie in prison. Put me in prison. Kill Jennifer with the disgrace of it all. And then, when youve done all the mischief you can, go to church and feel good about it. [*He sits down pettishly on the old chair at the easel, and takes up a sketching block, on which he begins to draw*].

WALPOLE. He's got us.

SIR PATRICK [*grimly*] He has.

B. B. But is he to be allowed to defy the criminal law of the land?

SIR PATRICK. The criminal law is no use to decent people. It only helps blackguards to blackmail their families. What are we family doctors doing half our time but conspiring with the family solicitor to keep some rascal out of jail and some family out of disgrace?

B. B. But at least it will punish him.

SIR PATRICK. Oh, yes: itll punish him. Itll punish not only him but everybody connected with him, innocent and guilty alike. Itll throw his board and lodging on our rates and taxes for a couple of years, and then turn him loose on us a more dangerous blackguard than ever. Itll put the girl in prison and ruin her: itll lay his wife's life waste. You may put the criminal law out of your head once for all: it's only fit for fools and savages.

LOUIS. Would you mind turning your face a little more this way, Sir Patrick. [*Sir Patrick turns indignantly and glares at him*]. Oh, thats too much.

SIR PATRICK. Put down your foolish pencil, man; and

147

THE DOCTOR'S DILEMMA

think of your position. You can defy the laws made by men; but there are other laws to reckon with. Do you know that youre going to die?

LOUIS. We're all going to die, arnt we?

WALPOLE. We're not all going to die in six months.

LOUIS. How do you know?

This for B. B. is the last straw. He completely loses his temper and begins to walk exitedly about.

B. B. Upon my soul, I will not stand this. It is in questionable taste under any circumstances or in any company to harp on the subject of death; but it is a dastardly advantage to take of a medical man. [*Thundering at Dubedat*] I will not allow it, do you hear?

LOUIS. Well, I didn't begin it: you chaps did. It's always the way with the inartistic professions: when theyre beaten in argument they fall back on intimidation. I never knew a lawyer who didnt threaten to put me in prison sooner or later. I never knew a parson who didnt threaten me with damnation. And now you threaten me with death. With all your talk youve only one real trump in your hand, and thats Intimidation. Well, I'm not a coward; so it's no use with me.

B. B. [*advancing upon him*] I'll tell you what you are, sir. Youre a scoundrel.

LOUIS. Oh, I don't mind you calling me a scoundrel a bit. It's only a word: a word that you dont know the meaning of. What is a scoundrel?

B. B. You are a scoundrel, sir.

LOUIS. Just so. What is a scoundrel? I am. What am I? A scoundrel. It's just arguing in a circle. And you imagine youre a man of science!

B. B. I—I—I—I have a good mind to take you by the scruff of your neck, you infamous rascal, and give you a sound thrashing.

LOUIS. I wish you would. Youd pay me something handsome to keep it out of court afterwards. [*B. B., baffled, flings away from him with a snort*]. Have you any more

148

civilities to address to me in my own house? I should like to get them over before my wife comes back. [*He resumes his sketching*].

RIDGEON. My mind's made up. When the law breaks down, honest men must find a remedy for themselves. I will not lift a finger to save this reptile.

B. B. That is the word I was trying to remember. Reptile.

WALPOLE. I cant help rather liking you, Dubedat. But you certainly are a thoroughgoing specimen.

SIR PATRICK. You know our opinion of you now, at all events.

LOUIS [*patiently putting down his pencil*] Look here. All this is no good. You dont understand. You imagine that I'm simply an ordinary criminal.

WALPOLE. Not an ordinary one, Dubedat. Do yourself justice.

LOUIS. Well youre on the wrong tack altogether. I'm not a criminal. All your moralizings have no value for me. I don't believe in morality. I'm a disciple of Bernard Shaw.

SIR PATRICK   [*puzzled*] Eh?

B. B.   [*waving his hand as if the subject were now disposed of*] Thats enough: I wish to hear no more.

LOUIS. Of course I havnt the ridiculous vanity to set up to be exactly a Superman; but still, it's an ideal that I strive towards just as any other man strives towards his ideal.

B. B. [*intolerant*] Dont trouble to explain. I now understand you perfectly. Say no more, please. When a man pretends to discuss science, morals, and religion, and then avows himself a follower of a notorious and avowed anti-vaccinationist, there is nothing more to be said. [*Suddenly putting in an effusive saving clause in parenthesis to Ridgeon*] Not, my dear Ridgeon, that I believe in vaccination in the popular sense any more than you do: I neednt tell you that. But there are things that place a man socially; and anti-vaccination is one of them. [*He resumes his seat*

149

on the dais].

SIR PATRICK. Bernard Shaw? I never heard of him. He's a Methodist preacher, I suppose.

LOUIS [*scandalized*] No, no. He's the most advanced man now living: he isn't anything.

SIR PATRICK. I assure you, young man, my father learnt the doctrine of deliverance from sin from John Wesley's own lips before you or Mr. Shaw were born. It used to be very popular as an excuse for putting sand in sugar and water in milk. Youre a sound Methodist, my lad; only you don't know it.

LOUIS [*seriously annoyed for the first time*] It's an intellectual insult. I don't believe theres such a thing as sin.

SIR PATRICK. Well, sir, there are people who dont believe theres such a thing as disease either. They call themselves Christian Scientists, I believe. Theyll just suit your complaint. We can do nothing for you. [*He rises*]. Good afternoon to you.

LOUIS [*running to him piteously*] Oh dont get up, Sir Patrick. Don't go. Please dont. I didnt mean to shock you, on my word. Do sit down again. Give me another chance. Two minutes more: thats all I ask.

SIR PATRICK [*surprised by this sign of grace, and a little touched*] Well— [*He sits down*]—

LOUIS [*gratefully*] Thanks awfully.

SIR PATRICK [*continuing*] —I don't mind giving you two minutes more. But dont address yourself to me; for Ive retired from practice; and I dont pretend to be able to cure your complaint. Your life is in the hands of these gentlemen.

RIDGEON. Not in mine. My hands are full. I have no time and no means available for this case.

SIR PATRICK. What do you say, Mr. Walpole?

WALPOLE. Oh, I'll take him in hand: I dont mind. I feel perfectly convinced that this is not a moral case at all: it's a physical one. Theres something abnormal about his brain. That means, probably, some morbid condition af-

THE DOCTOR'S DILEMMA

fecting the spinal cord. And that means the circulation. In short, it's clear to me that he's suffering from an obscure form of blood-poisoning, which is almost certainly due to an accumulation of ptomaines in the nuciform sac. I'll remove the sac—

LOUIS [*changing color*] Do you mean, operate on me? Ugh! No, thank you.

WALPOLE. Never fear: you wont feel anything. Youll be under an anæsthetic, of course. And it will be extraordinarily interesting.

LOUIS. Oh, well, if it would interest you, and if it wont hurt, thats another matter. How much will you give me to let you do it?

WALPOLE [*rising indignantly*] How much! What do you mean?

LOUIS. Well, you don't expect me to let you cut me up for nothing, do you?

WALPOLE. Will you paint my portrait for nothing?

LOUIS. No; but I'll give you the portrait when it's painted; and you can sell it afterwards for perhaps double the money. But I cant sell my nuciform sac when youve cut it out.

WALPOLE. Ridgeon: did you ever hear anything like this! [*To Louis*] Well, you can keep your nuciform sac, and your tubercular lung, and your diseased brain: Ive done with you. One would think I was not conferring a favor on the fellow! [*He returns to his stool in high dudgeon*].

SIR PATRICK. That leaves only one medical man who has not withdrawn from your case, Mr Dubedat. You have nobody left to appeal to now but Sir Ralph Bloomfield Bonington.

WALPOLE. If I were you, B. B., I shouldnt touch him with a pair of tongs. Let him take his lungs to the Brompton Hospital. They wont cure him; but theyll teach him manners.

B. B. My weakness is that I have never been able to say

151

THE DOCTOR'S DILEMMA

No, even to the most thoroughly undeserving people. Besides, I am bound to say that I dont think it is possible in medical practice to go into the question of the value of the lives we save. Just consider, Ridgeon. Let me put it to you, Paddy. Clear your mind of cant, Walpole.

WALPOLE [*indignantly*] My mind is clear of cant.

B. B. Quite so. Well now, look at my practice. It is what I suppose you would call a fashionable practice, a smart practice, a practice among the best people. You ask me to go into the question of whether my patients are of any use either to themselves or anyone else. Well, if you apply any scientific test known to me, you will achieve a reductio ad absurdum. You will be driven to the conclusion that the majority of them would be, as my friend Mr J. M. Barrie has tersely phrased it, better dead. Better dead. There are exceptions, no doubt. For instance, there is the court, an essentially social-democratic institution, supported out of public funds by the public because the public wants it and likes it. My court patients are hard-working people who give satisfaction, undoubtedly. Then I have a duke or two whose estates are probably better managed than they would be in public hands. But as to most of the rest, if I once began to argue about them, unquestionably the verdict would be, Better dead. When they actually do die, I sometimes have to offer that consolation, thinly disguised, to the family. [*Lulled by the cadences of his own voice, he becomes drowsier and drowsier*]. The fact that they spend money so extravagantly on medical attendance really would not justify me in wasting my talents—such as they are—in keeping them alive. After all, if my fees are high, I have to spend heavily. My own tastes are simple: a camp bed, a couple of rooms, a crust, a bottle of wine; and I am happy and contented. My wife's tastes are perhaps more luxurious; but even she deplores an expenditure the sole object of which is to maintain the state my patients require from their medical attendant. The—er—er—er— [*suddenly waking up*] I have lost the thread of these remarks. What

152

THE DOCTOR'S DILEMMA

was I talking about, Ridgeon?

RIDGEON. About Dubedat.

B. B. Ah yes. Precisely. Thank you. Dubedat, of course. Well, what is our friend Dubedat? A vicious and ignorant young man with a talent for drawing.

LOUIS. Thank you. Dont mind me.

B. B. But then, what are many of my patients? Vicious and ignorant young men without a talent for anything. If I were to stop to argue about their merits I should have to give up three-quarters of my practice. Therefore I have made it a rule not so to argue. Now, as an honorable man, having made that rule as to paying patients, can I make an exception as to a patient who, far from being a paying patient, may more fitly be described as a borrowing patient? No. I say No. Mr Dubedat: your moral character is nothing to me. I look at you from a purely scientific point of view. To me you are simply a field of battle in which an invading army of tubercle bacilli struggles with a patriotic force of phagocytes. Having made a promise to your wife, which my principles will not allow me to break, to stimulate those phagocytes, I will stimulate them. And I take no further responsibility. [*He flings himself back in his seat exhausted*].

SIR PATRICK. Well, Mr Dubedat, as Sir Ralph has very kindly offered to take charge of your case, and as the two minutes I promised you are up, I must ask you to excuse me. [*He rises*].

LOUIS. Oh, certainly. Ive quite done with you. [*Rising and holding up the sketch block*] There! While youve been talking, Ive been doing. What is there left of your moralizing? Only a little carbonic acid gas which makes the room unhealthy. What is there left of my work? That. Look at it [*Ridgeon rises to look at it*].

SIR PATRICK [*who has come down to him from the throne*] You young rascal, was it drawing me you were?

LOUIS. Of course. What else?

SIR PATRICK [*takes the drawing from him and grunts approvingly*] Thats rather good. Dont you think so, Colly?

153

RIDGEON. Yes. So good that I should like to have it.

SIR PATRICK. Thank you; but I should like to have it myself. What d'ye think, Walpole?

WALPOLE [*rising and coming over to look*] No, by Jove: *I* must have this.

LOUIS. I wish I could afford to give it to you, Sir Patrick. But I'd pay five guineas sooner than part with it.

RIDGEON. Oh, for that matter, I will give you six for it.

WALPOLE. Ten.

LOUIS. I think Sir Patrick is morally entitled to it, as he sat for it. May I send it to your house, Sir Patrick, for twelve guineas?

SIR PATRICK. Twelve guineas! Not if you were President of the Royal Academy, young man. [*He gives him back the drawing decisively and turns away, taking up his hat*].

LOUIS [*to B. B.*] Would you like to take it at twelve, Sir Ralph?

B. B. [*coming between Louis and Walpole*] Twelve guineas? Thank you: I'll take it at that. [*He takes it and presents it to Sir Patrick*]. Accept it from me, Paddy; and may you long be spared to contemplate it.

SIR PATRICK. Thank you. [*He puts the drawing into his hat*].

B. B. I neednt settle with you now, Mr Dubedat: my fees will come to more than that. [*He also retrieves his hat*].

LOUIS [*indignantly*] Well, of all the mean—[*words fail him*]! I'd let myself be shot sooner than do a thing like that. I consider youve stolen that drawing.

SIR PATRICK [*drily*] So weve converted you to a belief in morality after all, eh?

LOUIS. Yah! [*To Walpole*] I'll do another one for you, Walpole, if youll let me have the ten you promised.

WALPOLE. Very good. I'll pay on delivery.

LOUIS. Oh! What do you take me for? Have you no confidence in my honor?

WALPOLE. None whatever.

LOUIS. Oh well, of course if you feel that way, you cant help it. Before you go, Sir Patrick, let me fetch Jennifer. I know she'd like to see you, if you dont mind. [*He goes to the inner door*]. And now, before she comes in, one word. Youve all been talking here pretty freely about me—in my own house too. *I* dont mind that: I'm a man and can take care of myself. But when Jennifer comes in, please remember that she's a lady, and that you are supposed to be gentlemen. [*He goes out*].

WALPOLE. Well!!! [*He gives the situation up as indescribable, and goes for his hat*].

RIDGEON. Damn his impudence!

B. B. I shouldnt be at all surprised to learn that he's well connected. Whenever I meet dignity and self-possession without any discoverable basis, I diagnose good family.

RIDGEON. Diagnose artistic genius, B. B. Thats what saves his self-respect.

SIR PATRICK. The world is made like that. The decent fellows are always being lectured and put out of countenance by the snobs.

B. B. [*altogether refusing to accept this*] I am not out of countenance. I should like, by Jupiter, to see the man who could put me out of countenance. [*Jennifer comes in*]. Ah, Mrs Dubedat! And how are we to-day?

MRS DUBEDAT [*shaking hands with him*] Thank you all so much for coming. [*She shakes Walpole's hand*]. Thank you, Sir Patrick [*she shakes Sir Patrick's*]. Oh, life has been worth living since I have known you. Since Richmond I have not known a moment's fear. And it used to be nothing but fear. Wont you sit down and tell me the result of the consultation?

WALPOLE. I'll go, if you dont mind, Mrs Dubedat. I have an appointment. Before I go, let me say that I am quite agreed with my colleagues here as to the character of the case. As to the cause and the remedy, thats not my business: I'm only a surgeon; and these gentlemen are physicians and will advise you. I may have my own views: in fact

I h a v e them; and they are perfectly well known to my colleagues. If I am needed—and needed I shall be finally —they know where to find me; and I am always at your service. So for to-day, good-bye. [*He goes out, leaving Jennifer much puzzled by his unexpected withdrawal and formal manner*].

SIR PATRICK. I also will ask you to excuse me, Mrs Dubedat.

RIDGEON [*anxiously*] Are you going?

SIR PATRICK. Yes: I can be of no use here; and I must be getting back. As you know, maam, I'm not in practice now; and I shall not be in charge of the case. It rests between Sir Colenso Ridgeon and Sir Ralph Bloomfield Bonington. They know my opinion. Good afternoon to you, maam. [*He bows and makes for the door*].

MRS DUBEDAT [*detaining him*] Theres nothing wrong, is there? You dont think Louis is worse, do you?

SIR PATRICK. No: he's not worse. Just the same as at Richmond.

MRS DUBEDAT. Oh, thank you: you frightened me. Excuse me.

SIR PATRICK. Dont mention it, maam. [*He goes out*].

B. B. Now, Mrs Dubedat, if I am to take the patient in hand—

MRS DUBEDAT [*apprehensively, with a glance at Ridgeon*] You! But I thought that Sir Colenso—

B. B. [*beaming with the conviction that he is giving her a most gratifying surprise*] My dear lady, your husband shall have Me.

MRS DUBEDAT. But—

B. B. Not a word: it is a pleasure to me, for your sake. Sir Colenso Ridgeon will be in his proper place, in the bacteriological laboratory. *I* shall be in my proper place, at the bedside. Your husband shall be treated exactly as if he were a member of the royal family. [*Mrs Dubedat uneasy, again is about to protest*]. No gratitude: it would embarrass me, I assure you. Now, may I ask whether you are particularly

156

Mrs. Dubedat. "I know I ought to be very grateful. Believe me, I am very grateful. But—but—"

Katharine Cornell and Raymond Massey

tied to these apartments. Of course, the motor has annihilated distance; but I confess that if you were rather nearer to me, it would be a l i t t l e more convenient.

MRS DUBEDAT. You see, this studio and flat are self-contained. I have suffered so much in lodgings. The servants are so frightfully dishonest.

B. B. Ah! Are they? Are they? Dear me!

MRS DUBEDAT. I was never accustomed to lock things up. And I missed so many small sums. At last a dreadful thing happened. I missed a five-pound note. It was traced to the housemaid; and she actually said Louis had given it to her. And he wouldnt let me do anything: he is so sensitive that these things drive him mad.

. B. B. Ah—hm—ha—yes—say no more, Mrs Dubedat: you shall not move. If the mountain will not come to Mahomet, Mahomet must come to the mountain. Now I must be off. I will write and make an appointment. We shall begin stimulating the phagocytes on—on—probably on Tuesday next; but I will let you know. Depend on me; dont fret; eat regularly; sleep well; keep your spirits up; keep the patient cheerful; hope for the best; no tonic like a charming woman; no medicine like cheerfulness; no resource like science; good-bye, good-bye, good-bye. [*Having shaken hands—she being too overwhelmed to speak—he goes out, stopping to say to Ridgeon*] On Tuesday morning send me down a tube of some really stiff anti-toxin. Any kind will do. Dont forget. Good-bye, Colly. [*He goes out*].

RIDGEON. You look quite discouraged again. [*She is almost in tears*]. What's the matter? Are you disappointed?

MRS DUBEDAT. I know I ought to be very grateful. Believe me, I am very grateful. But—but—

RIDGEON. Well?

MRS DUBEDAT. I had set my heart on y o u r curing Louis.

RIDGEON. Well, Sir Ralph Bloomfield Bonington—

MRS DUBEDAT. Yes, I know, I know. It is a great privilege to have him. But oh, I wish it had been you. I know it's unreasonable; I cant explain; but I had such a strong instinct that you would cure him. I dont—I cant feel the same about Sir Ralph. You promised me. Why did you give Louis up?

RIDGEON. I explained to you. I cannot take another case.

MRS DUBEDAT. But at Richmond?

RIDGEON. At Richmond I thought I could make room for one more case. But my old friend Dr Blenkinsop claimed that place. His lung is attacked.

MRS DUBEDAT [*attaching no importance whatever to Blenkinsop*] Do you mean that elderly man—that rather silly—

RIDGEON [*sternly*] I mean the gentleman that dined with us: an excellent and honest man, whose life is as valuable as anyone else's. I have arranged that I shall take his case, and that Sir Ralph Bloomfield Bonington shall take Mr Dubedat's.

MRS DUBEDAT [*turning indignantly on him*] I see what it is. Oh! it is envious, mean, cruel. And I thought that you would be above such a thing.

RIDGEON. What do you mean?

MRS DUBEDAT. Oh, do you think I dont know? do you think it has never happened before? Why does everybody turn against him? Can you not forgive him for being superior to you? for being cleverer? for being braver? for being a great artist?

RIDGEON. Yes: I can forgive him for all that.

MRS DUBEDAT. Well, have you anything to say against him? I have challenged everyone who has turned against him—challenged them face to face to tell me any wrong thing he has done, any ignoble thought he has uttered. They have always confessed that they could not tell me one. I challenge you now. What do you accuse him of?

RIDGEON. I am like all the rest. Face to face, I cannot tell you one thing against him.

MRS DUBEDAT [*not satisfied*] But your manner is changed. And you have broken your promise to me to make

158

room for him as your patient.

RIDGEON. I think you are a little unreasonable. You have had the very best medical advice in London for him; and his case has been taken in hand by a leader of the profession. Surely—

MRS DUBEDAT. Oh, it is so cruel to keep telling me that. It seems all right; and it puts me in the wrong. But I am not in the wrong. I have faith in you; and I have no faith in the others. We have seen so many doctors: I have come to know at last when they are only talking and can do nothing. It is different with you. I feel that you know. You must listen to me, doctor. [*With sudden misgiving*] Am I offending you by calling you doctor instead of remembering your title?

RIDGEON. Nonsense. I a m a doctor. But mind you, dont call Walpole one.

MRS DUBEDAT. I dont care about Mr Walpole: it is you who must befriend me. Oh, will you please sit down and listen to me just for a few minutes. [*He assents with a grave inclination, and sits on the sofa. She sits on the easel chair*]. Thank you. I wont keep you long; but I must tell you the whole truth. Listen. I know Louis as nobody else in the world knows him or ever can know him. I am his wife. I know he has little faults: impatiences, sensitivenesses, even little selfishnesses that are too trivial for him to notice. I know that he sometimes shocks people about money because he is so utterly above it, and cant understand the value ordinary people set on it. Tell me: did he—did he borrow any money from you?

RIDGEON. He asked me for some—once.

MRS DUBEDAT [*tears again in her eyes*] Oh, I am so sorry—so sorry. But he will never do it again: I pledge you my word for that. He has given me his promise: here in this room just before you came; and he is incapable of breaking his word. That was his only real weakness; and now it is conquered and done with for ever.

RIDGEON. Was that really his only weakness?

159

MRS DUBEDAT. He is perhaps sometimes weak about women, because they adore him so, and are always laying traps for him. And of course when he says he doesnt believe in morality, ordinary pious people think he must be wicked. You can understand, cant you, how all this starts a great deal of gossip about him, and gets repeated until even good friends get set against him?

RIDGEON. Yes: I understand.

MRS DUBEDAT. Oh, if you only knew the other side of him as I do! Do you know, doctor, that if Louis dishonored himself by a really bad action, I should kill myself.

RIDGEON. Come! dont exaggerate.

MRS DUBEDAT. I should. You dont understand that, you east country people.

RIDGEON. You did not see much of the world in Cornwall, did you?

MRS DUBEDAT [*naïvely*] Oh yes. I saw a great deal every day of the beauty of the world—more than you ever see here in London. But I saw very few people, if that is what you mean. I was an only child.

RIDGEON. That explains a good deal.

MRS DUBEDAT. I had a great many dreams; but at last they all came to one dream.

RIDGEON [*with half a sigh*] Yes, the usual dream.

MRS DUBEDAT [*surprised*] Is it usual?

RIDGEON. As I guess. You havnt yet told me what it was.

MRS DUBEDAT. I didn't want to waste myself. I could do nothing myself; but I had a little property and I could help with it. I had even a little beauty: dont think me vain for knowing it. I knew that men of genius always had a terrible struggle with poverty and neglect at first. My dream was to save one of them from that, and bring some charm and happiness into his life. I prayed Heaven to send me one. I firmly believe that Louis was guided to me in answer to my prayer. He was no more like the other men I had met than the Thames Embankment is like our Cornish coasts.

160

THE DOCTOR'S DILEMMA

He saw everything that I saw, and drew it for me. He understood everything. He came to me like a child. Only fancy, doctor: he never even wanted to marry me: he never thought of the things other men think of! I had to propose it myself. Then he said he had no money. When I told him I had some, he said "Oh, all right," just like a boy. He is still like that, quite unspoiled, a man in his thoughts, a great poet and artist in his dreams, and a child in his ways. I gave him myself and all I had that he might grow to his full height with plenty of sunshine. If I lost faith in him, it would mean the wreck and failure of my life. I should go back to Cornwall and die. I could show you the very cliff I should jump off. You must cure him: you must make him quite well again for me. I know that you can do it and that nobody else can. I implore you not to refuse what I am going to ask you to do. Take Louis yourself; and let Sir Ralph cure Dr Blenkinsop.

RIDGEON [*slowly*] Mrs Dubedat: do you really believe in my knowledge and skill as you say you do?

MRS DUBEDAT. Absolutely. I do not give my trust by halves.

RIDGEON. I know that. Well, I am going to test you— hard. Will you believe me when I tell you that I understand what you have just told me; that I have no desire but to serve you in the most faithful friendship; and that your hero must be preserved to you.

MRS DUBEDAT. Oh forgive me. Forgive what I said. You will preserve him to me.

RIDGEON. At all hazards. [*She kisses his hand. He rises hastily*]. N o: you have not heard the rest. [*She rises too*]. You must believe me when I tell you that the one chance of preserving the hero lies in Louis being in the care of Sir Ralph.

MRS DUBEDAT [*firmly*] You say so: I have no more doubt: I believe you. Thank you.

RIDGEON. Good-bye. [*She takes his hand*]. I hope this

161

will be a lasting friendship.

MRS DUBEDAT. It will. My friendships end only with death.

RIDGEON. Death ends everything, doesnt it? Good-bye.

With a sigh and a look of pity at her which she does not understand, he goes.

ACT IV

THE studio. The easel is pushed back to the wall. Cardinal Death, holding his scythe and hour-glass like a sceptre and globe, sits on the throne. On the hat-stand hang the hats of Sir Patrick and Bloomfield Bonington. Walpole, just come in, is hanging up his beside them. There is a knock. He opens the door and finds Ridgeon there.

WALPOLE. Hallo, Ridgeon!
They come into the middle of the room together, taking off their gloves.
RIDGEON. Whats the matter! Have you been sent for, too?
WALPOLE. Weve all been sent for. Ive only just come: I havnt seen him yet. The charwoman says that old Paddy Cullen has been here with B. B. for the last half-hour. [*Sir Patrick, with bad news in his face, enters from the inner room*]. Well: whats up?
SIR PATRICK. Go in and see. B. B. is in there with him.
Walpole goes. Ridgeon is about to follow him; but Sir Patrick stops him with a look.
RIDGEON. What has happened?
SIR PATRICK. Do you remember Jane Marsh's arm?
RIDGEON. Is that whats happened?
SIR PATRICK. Thats whats happened. His lung has gone like Jane's arm. I never saw such a case. He has got through three months galloping consumption in three days.
RIDGEON. B. B. got in on the negative phase.
SIR PATRICK. Negative or positive, the lad's done for. He wont last out the afternoon. He'll go suddenly: Ive often seen it.
RIDGEON. So long as he goes before his wife finds him out, *I* don't care. I fully expected this.
SIR PATRICK [*drily*] It's a little hard on a lad to be killed because his wife has too high an opinion of him. Fortunately few of us are in any danger of that.

163

THE DOCTOR'S DILEMMA

Sir Ralph comes from the inner room and hastens between them, humanely concerned, but professionally elate and communicative.

B. B. Ah, here you are, Ridgeon. Paddy's told you, of course.

RIDGEON. Yes.

B. B. It's an enormously interesting case. You know, Colly, by Jupiter, if I didnt know as a matter of scientific fact that I'd been stimulating the phagocytes, I should say I'd been stimulating the other things. What is the explanation of it, Sir Patrick? How do you account for it, Ridgeon? Have we over-stimulated the phagocytes? Have they not only eaten up the bacilli, but attacked and destroyed the red corpuscles as well? a possibility suggested by the patient's pallor. Nay, have they finally begun to prey on the lungs themselves? Or on one another? I shall write a paper about this case.

Walpole comes back, very serious, even shocked. He comes between B. B. and Ridgeon.

WALPOLE. Whew! B. B.: youve done it this time.

B. B. What do you mean?

WALPOLE. Killed him. The worst case of neglected blood-poisoning I ever saw. It's too late now to do anything. He'd die under the anæsthetic.

B. B. [*offended*] Killed! Really, Walpole, if your monomania were not well known, I should take such an expression very seriously.

SIR PATRICK. Come come! When youve both killed as many people as I have in my time youll feel humble enough about it. Come and look at him, Colly.

Ridgeon and Sir Patrick go into the inner room.

WALPOLE. I apologize, B. B. But it's blood-poisoning.

B. B. [*recovering his irresistible good nature*] My dear Walpole, e v e r y t h i n g is blood-poisoning. But upon my soul, I shall not use any of that stuff of Ridgeon's again. What made me so sensitive about what you said just now is that, strictly between ourselves, Ridgeon has cooked our young friend's goose.

Jennifer, worried and distressed, but always gentle, comes between them from the inner room. She wears a nurse's apron.

MRS DUBEDAT. Sir Ralph: what am I to do? That man who insisted on seeing me, and sent in word that his business was important to Louis, is a newspaper man. A paragraph appeared in the paper this morning saying that Louis is seriously ill; and this man wants to interview him about it. How can people be so brutally callous?

WALPOLE [*moving vengefully towards the door*] You just leave me to deal with him!

MRS DUBEDAT [*stopping him*] But Louis insists on seeing him: he almost began to cry about it. And he says he cant bear his room any longer. He says he wants to [*she struggles with a sob*]—to die in his studio. Sir Patrick says let him have his way: it can do no harm. What shall we do?

B. B. [*encouragingly*] Why, follow Sir Patrick's excellent advice, of course. As he says, it can do him no harm; and it will no doubt do him good—a great deal of good. He will be much the better for it.

MRS DUBEDAT [*a little cheered*] Will you bring the man up here, Mr Walpole, and tell him that he may see Louis, but that he mustnt exhaust him by talking? [*Walpole nods and goes out by the outer door*]. Sir Ralph, dont be angry with me; but Louis will die if he stays here. I must take him to Cornwall. He will recover there.

B. B. [*brightening wonderfully, as if Dubedat were already saved*] Cornwall! The very place for him! Wonderful for the lungs. Stupid of me not to think of it before. You are his best physician after all, dear lady. An inspiration! Cornwall: of course, yes, yes, yes.

MRS DUBEDAT [*comforted and touched*] You are so kind, Sir Ralph. But dont give me m u c h or I shall cry; and Louis cant bear that.

B. B. [*gently putting his protecting arm round her shoulders*] Then let us come back to him and help to carry

165

him in. Cornwall! of course, of course. The very thing!
[*They go together into the bedroom*].

*Walpole returns with The Newspaper Man, a cheerful,
affable young man who is disabled for ordinary business
pursuits by a congenital erroneousness which renders him
incapable of describing accurately anything he sees or understanding or reporting accurately anything he hears. As
the only employment in which these defects do not matter
is journalism (for a newspaper, not having to act on its
description and reports, but only to sell them to idly curious
people, has nothing but honor to lose by inaccuracy and un-
veracity), he has perforce become a journalist, and has to
keep up an air of high spirits through a daily struggle with
his own illiteracy and the precariousness of his employment.
He has a note-book, and occasionally attempts to make a
note; but as he cannot write shorthand, and does not write
with ease in any hand, he generally gives it up as a bad job
before he succeeds in finishing a sentence.*

THE NEWSPAPER MAN [*looking round and making in-
decisive attempts at notes*] This is the studio, I suppose.

WALPOLE. Yes.

THE NEWSPAPER MAN [*wittily*] Where he has his
models, eh?

WALPOLE [*grimly irresponsive*] No doubt.

THE NEWSPAPER MAN. Cubicle, you said it was?

WALPOLE. Yes, tubercle.

THE NEWSPAPER MAN. Which way do you spell it: is it
c-u-b-i-c-a-l or c-l-e?

WALPOLE. Tubercle, man, not cubical. [*Spelling it for
him*] T-u-b-e-r-c-l-e.

THE NEWSPAPER MAN. Oh! tubercle. Some disease, I
suppose. I thought he had consumption. Are you one of the
family or the doctor?

WALPOLE. I'm neither one nor the other. I am M i s t e r
Cutler Walpole. Put that down. Then put down Sir Colenso
Ridgeon.

THE NEWSPAPER MAN. Pigeon?

THE DOCTOR'S DILEMMA

WALPOLE. Ridgeon. [*Contemptuously snatching his book*] Here: youd better let me write the names down for you: youre sure to get them wrong. That comes of belonging to an illiterate profession, with no qualifications and no public register. [*He writes the particulars*].

THE NEWSPAPER MAN. Oh, I say: you h a v e got your knife into us, havnt you?

WALPOLE [*vindictively*] I wish I had: I'd make a better man of you. Now attend. [*Shewing him the book*] These are the names of the three doctors. This is the patient. This is the address. This is the name of the disease. [*He shuts the book with a snap which makes the journalist blink, and returns it to him*]. Mr Dubedat will be brought in here presently. He wants to see you because he doesnt know how bad he is. We'll allow you to wait a few minutes to humor him; but if you talk to him, out you go. He may die at any moment.

THE NEWSPAPER MAN [*interested*] Is he as bad as that? I say: I a m in luck to-day. Would you mind letting me photograph you? [*He produces a camera*]. Could you have a lancet or something in your hand?

WALPOLE. Put it up. If you want my photograph you can get it in Baker Street in any of the series of celebrities.

THE NEWSPAPER MAN. But theyll want to be paid. If you wouldnt mind [*fingering the camera*]—?

WALPOLE. I would. Put it up, I tell you. Sit down there and be quiet.

The Newspaper Man quickly sits down on the piano stool as Dubedat, in an invalid's chair, is wheeled in by Mrs Dubedat and Sir Ralph. They place the chair between the dais and the sofa, where the easel stood before. Louis is not changed as a robust man would be; and he is not scared. His eyes look larger; and he is so weak physically that he can hardly move, lying on his cushions with complete languor; but his mind is active; it is making the most of his condition, finding voluptuousness in languor and drama in death. They are all impressed, in spite of themselves, except

167

THE DOCTOR'S DILEMMA

*Ridgeon, who is implacable. B. B. is entirely sympathetic
and forgiving. Ridgeon follows the chair with a tray of milk
and stimulants. Sir Patrick, who accompanies him, takes the
tea-table from the corner and places it behind the chair for
the tray. B. B. takes the easel chair and places it for Jennifer
at Dubedat's side, next the dais, from which the lay figure
ogles the dying artist. B. B. then returns to Dubedat's left.
Jennifer sits. Walpole sits down on the edge of the dais.
Ridgeon stands near him.*

LOUIS [*blissfully*] Thats happiness. To be in a studio!
Happiness!

MRS DUBEDAT. Yes, dear. Sir Patrick says you may stay
here as long as you like.

LOUIS. Jennifer.

MRS DUBEDAT. Yes, my darling.

LOUIS. Is the newspaper man here?

THE NEWSPAPER MAN [*glibly*] Yes, Mr Dubedat: I'm
here, at your service. I represent the press. I thought you
might like to let us have a few words about—about—er—
well, a few words on your illness, and your plans for the
season.

LOUIS. My plans for the season are very simple. I'm going to die.

MRS DUBEDAT [*tortured*] Louis—dearest—

LOUIS. My darling: I'm very weak and tired. Dont put
on me the horrible strain of pretending that I dont know.
Ive been lying there listening to the doctors—laughing to
myself. They know. Dearest: dont cry. It makes you ugly;
and I cant bear that. [*She dries her eyes and recovers herself with a proud effort*]. I want you to promise me something.

MRS DUBEDAT. Yes, yes: you know I will. [*Implor-
ingly*] Only, my love, my love, dont talk: it will waste your
strength.

LOUIS. No: it will only use it up. Ridgeon: give me
something to keep me going for a few minutes—not one of
your confounded anti-toxins, if you dont mind. I have some

168

THE DOCTOR'S DILEMMA

things to say before I go.

RIDGEON [*looking at Sir Patrick*] I suppose it can do no harm? [*He pours out some spirit, and is about to add soda water when Sir Patrick corrects him*].

SIR PATRICK. In milk. Dont set him coughing.

LOUIS [*after drinking*] Jennifer.

MRS DUBEDAT. Yes, dear.

LOUIS. If theres one thing I hate more than another, it's a widow. Promise me that youll never be a widow.

MRS DUBEDAT. My dear, what do you mean?

LOUIS. I want you to look beautiful. I want people to see in your eyes that you were married to me. The people in Italy used to point at Dante and say "There goes the man who has been in hell." I want them to point at you and say "There goes a woman who has been in heaven." It h a s been heaven, darling, hasnt it—sometimes?

MRS DUBEDAT. Oh yes, yes. Always, always.

LOUIS. If you wear black and cry, people will say "Look at that miserable woman: her husband made her miserable."

MRS DUBEDAT. No, never. You are the light and the blessing of my life. I never lived until I knew you.

LOUIS [*his eyes glistening*] Then you must always wear beautiful dresses and splendid magic jewels. Think of all the wonderful pictures I shall never paint. [*She wins a terrible victory over a sob*] Well, you must be transfigured with all the beauty of those pictures. Men must get such dreams from seeing you as they never could get from any daubing with paints and brushes. Painters must paint you as they never painted any mortal woman before. There must be a great tradition of beauty, a great atmosphere of wonder and romance. That is what men must always think of when they think of me. That is the sort of immortality I want. You can make that for me, Jennifer. There are lots of things you dont understand that every woman in the street understands; but you can understand that and do it as nobody else can. Promise me that immortality. Promise me you will not make a little hell of crape and crying and

169

undertaker's horrors and withering flowers and all that vulgar rubbish.

MRS DUBEDAT. I promise. But all that is far off, dear. You are to come to Cornwall with me and get well. Sir Ralph says so.

LOUIS. Poor old B. B.

B. B. [*affected to tears, turns away and whispers to Sir Patrick*] Poor fellow! Brain going.

LOUIS. Sir Patrick's there, isnt he?

SIR PATRICK. Yes, yes. I'm here.

LOUIS. Sit down, wont you? It's a shame to keep you standing about.

SIR PATRICK. Yes, yes. Thank you. All right.

LOUIS. Jennifer.

MRS DUBEDAT. Yes, dear.

LOUIS [*with a strange look of delight*] Do you remember the burning bush?

MRS DUBEDAT. Yes, yes. Oh, my dear, how it strains my heart to remember it now!

LOUIS. Does it? It fills me with joy. Tell them about it.

MRS DUBEDAT. It was nothing—only that once in my old Cornish home we lit the first fire of the winter; and when we looked through the window we saw the flames dancing in a bush in the garden.

LOUIS. Such a color! Garnet color. Waving like silk. Liquid lovely flame flowing up through the bay leaves, and not burning them. Well, I shall be a flame like that. I'm sorry to disappoint the poor little worms; but the last of me shall be the flame in the burning bush. Whenever you see the flame, Jennifer, that will be me. Promise me that I shall be burnt.

MRS DUBEDAT. Oh, if I might be with you, Louis!

LOUIS. No: you must always be in the garden when the bush flames. You are my hold on the world: you are my immortality. Promise.

MRS DUBEDAT. I'm listening. I shall not forget. You know that I promise.

170

THE DOCTOR'S DILEMMA

LOUIS. Well, thats about all; except that you are to hang my pictures at the one-man-show. I can trust your eye. You wont let anyone else touch them.

MRS DUBEDAT. You can trust me.

LOUIS. Then theres nothing more to worry about, is there? Give me some more of that milk. I'm fearfully tired; but if I stop talking I shant begin again. [*Sir Ralph gives him a drink. He takes it and looks up quaintly*]. I say, B. B., do you think anything would stop y o u talking?

B. B. [*almost unmanned*] He confuses me with you, Paddy. Poor fellow! Poor fellow!

LOUIS [*musing*] I used to be awfully afraid of death; but now it's come I have no fear; and I'm perfectly happy. Jennifer.

MRS DUBEDAT. Yes, dear?

LOUIS. I'll tell you a secret. I used to think that our marriage was all an affectation, and that I'd break loose and run away some day. But now that I'm going to be broken loose whether I like it or not, I'm perfectly fond of you, and perfectly satisfied because I'm going to live as part of you and not as my troublesome self.

MRS DUBEDAT [*heartbroken*] Stay with me, Louis. Oh, dont leave me, dearest.

LOUIS. Not that I'm selfish. With all my faults I dont think Ive ever been really selfish. No artist can: Art is too large for that. You will marry again, Jennifer.

MRS DUBEDAT. Oh, how c a n you, Louis?

LOUIS [*insisting childishly*] Yes, because people who have found marriage happy always marry again. Ah, *I* shant be jealous. [*Slyly.*] But dont talk to the other fellow too much about me: he wont like it. [*Almost chuckling*] I shall be your lover all the time; but it will be a secret from him, poor devil!

SIR PATRICK. Come! youve talked enough. Try to rest awhile.

LOUIS [*wearily*] Yes: I'm fearfully tired; but I shall have a long rest presently. I have something to say to you

171

fellows. Youre all there, arnt you? I'm too weak to see anything but Jennifer's bosom. That promises rest.

RIDGEON. We are all here.

LOUIS [*startled*] That voice sounded devilish. Take care, Ridgeon: my ears hear things that other people's ears cant. Ive been thinking—thinking. I'm cleverer than you imagine.

SIR PATRICK [*whispering to Ridgeon*] Youve got on his nerves, Colly. Slip out quietly.

RIDGEON [*apart to Sir Patrick*] Would you deprive the dying actor of his audience?

LOUIS [*his face lighting up faintly with mischievous glee*] I heard that, Ridgeon. That was good. Jennifer, dear: be kind to Ridgeon always; because he was the last man who amused me.

RIDGEON [*relentless*] Was I?

LOUIS. But it's not true. It's you who are still on the stage. I'm half way home already.

MRS DUBEDAT [*to Ridgeon*] What did you say?

LOUIS [*answering for him*] Nothing, dear. Only one of those little secrets that men keep among themselves. Well, all you chaps have thought pretty hard things of me, and said them.

B. B. [*quite overcome*] No, no, Dubedat. Not at all.

LOUIS. Yes, you have. I know what you all think of me. Dont imagine I'm sore about it. I forgive you.

WALPOLE [*involuntarily*] Well, damn me! [*Ashamed*] I beg your pardon.

LOUIS. That was old Walpole, I know. Dont grieve, Walpole. I'm perfectly happy. I'm not in pain. I dont want to live. I've escaped from myself. I'm in heaven, immortal in the heart of my beautiful Jennifer. I'm not afraid, and not ashamed. [*Reflectively, puzzling it out for himself weakly*] I know that in an accidental sort of way, struggling through the unreal part of life, I havnt always been able to live up to my ideal. But in my own real world I have never done anything wrong, never denied my faith, never

172

Louis [*musing*] "I used to be awfully afraid of death; but now it's come I have no fear."

Katharine Cornell, Raymond Massey, Bramwell Fletcher, Ralph Forbes, Whitford Kane, Cecil Humphreys

been untrue to myself. Ive been threatened and blackmailed and insulted and starved. But Ive played the game. Ive fought the good fight. And now it's all over, theres an indescribable peace. [*He feebly folds his hands and utters his creed*] I believe in Michael Angelo, Velasquez, and Rembrandt; in the might of design, the mystery of color, the redemption of all things by Beauty everlasting, and the message of Art that has made these hands blessed. Amen. Amen. [*He closes his eyes and lies still*].

MRS DUBEDAT [*breathless*] Louis: are you—
Walpole rises and comes quickly to see whether he is dead.

LOUIS. Not yet, dear. Very nearly, but not yet. I should like to rest my head on your bosom; only it would tire you.

MRS DUBEDAT. No, no, no, darling: how could you tire me? [*She lifts him so that he lies on her bosom*].

LOUIS. Thats good. Thats real.

MRS DUBEDAT. Dont spare me, dear. Indeed, i n d e e d you will not tire me. Lean on me with all your weight.

LOUIS [*with a sudden half return of his normal strength and comfort*] Jinny Gwinny: I think I shall recover after all. [*Sir Patrick looks significantly at Ridgeon, mutely warning him that this is the end*].

MRS DUBEDAT [*hopefully*] Yes, yes: you shall.

LOUIS. Because I suddenly want to sleep. Just an ordinary sleep.

MRS DUBEDAT [*rocking him*] Yes, dear. Sleep. [*He seems to go to sleep. Walpole makes another movement. She protests*]. Sh-sh: please dont disturb him. [*His lips move*]. What did you say, dear? [*In great distress*] I cant listen without moving him. [*His lips move again: Walpole bends down and listens*].

WALPOLE. He wants to know is the newspaper man here.

THE NEWSPAPER MAN [*excited; for he has been enjoying himself enormously*] Yes, Mr Dubedat. Here I am.
Walpole raises his hand warningly to silence him. Sir

Ralph sits down quietly on the sofa and frankly buries his face in his handkerchief.

MRS DUBEDAT [*with great relief*] Oh thats right, dear: dont spare me: lean with all your weight on me. Now you are really resting.

Sir Patrick quickly comes forward and feels Louis's pulse; then takes him by the shoulders.

SIR PATRICK. Let me put him back on the pillow, maam. He will be better so.

MRS DUBEDAT [*piteously*] Oh no, please, p l e a s e, doctor. He is not tiring me; and he will be so hurt when he wakes if he finds I have put him away.

SIR PATRICK. He will never wake again. [*He takes the body from her and replaces it in the chair. Ridgeon, unmoved, lets down the back and makes a bier of it*].

MRS DUBEDAT [*who has unexpectedly sprung to her feet, and stands dry-eyed and stately*] Was that death?

WALPOLE. Yes.

MRS DUBEDAT [*with complete dignity*] Will you wait for me a moment? I will come back. [*She goes out*].

WALPOLE. Ought we to follow her? Is she in her right senses?

SIR PATRICK [*with quiet conviction*] Yes. Shes all right. Leave her alone. She'll come back.

RIDGEON [*callously*] Let us get this thing out of the way before she comes.

B. B. [*rising, shocked*] My dear Colly! The poor lad! He died splendidly.

SIR PATRICK. Aye! that is how the wicked die.

> For there are no bands in their death;
> But their strength is firm:
> They are not in trouble as other men.

No matter: it's not for us to judge. He's in another world now.

WALPOLE. Borrowing his first five-pound note there, probably.

RIDGEON. I said the other day that the most tragic thing in the world is a sick doctor. I was wrong. The most tragic thing in the world is a man of genius who is not also a man of honor.

Ridgeon and Walpole wheel the chair into the recess.

THE NEWSPAPER MAN [*to Sir Ralph*] I thought it shewed a very nice feeling, his being so particular about his wife going into proper mourning for him and making her promise never to marry again.

B. B. [*impressively*] Mrs Dubedat is not in a position to carry the interview any further. Neither are we.

SIR PATRICK. Good afternoon to you.

THE NEWSPAPER MAN. Mrs Dubedat said she was coming back.

B. B. After you have gone.

THE NEWSPAPER MAN. Do you think she would give me a few words on How It Feels to be a Widow? Rather a good title for an article, isnt it?

B. B. Young man: if you wait until Mrs Dubedat comes back, you will be able to write an article on How It Feels to be Turned Out of the House.

THE NEWSPAPER MAN [*unconvinced*] You think she'd rather not—

B. B. [*cutting him short*] Good day to you. [*Giving him a visiting-card*] Mind you get my name correctly. Good day.

THE NEWSPAPER MAN. Good day. Thank you. [*Vaguely trying to read the card*] Mr—

B. B. No, not Mister. This is your hat, I think [*giving it to him*]. Gloves? No, of course: no gloves. Good day to you. [*He edges him out at last; shuts the door on him; and returns to Sir Patrick as Ridgeon and Walpole come back from the recess, Walpole crossing the room to the hat-stand, and Ridgeon coming between Sir Ralph and Sir Patrick*]. Poor fellow! Poor young fellow! How well he died! I feel a better man, really.

SIR PATRICK. When youre as old as I am, youll know

that it matters very little how a man dies. What matters
is, how he lives. Every fool that runs his nose against a
bullet is a hero nowadays, because he dies for his country.
Why dont he live for it to some purpose?

B. B. No, please, Paddy: dont be hard on the poor lad.
Not now, not now. After all, was he so bad? He had only
two failings: money and women. Well, let us be honest.
Tell the truth, Paddy. Dont be hypocritical, Ridgeon.
Throw off the mask, Walpole. Are these two matters so
well arranged at present that a disregard of the usual arrangements indicates real depravity?

WALPOLE. I dont mind his disregarding the usual arrangements. Confound the usual arrangements! To a man
of science theyre beneath contempt both as to money and
women. What I mind is his disregarding everything except
his own pocket and his own fancy. He didnt disregard the
usual arrangements when they paid him. Did he give us
his pictures for nothing? Do you suppose he'd have hesi-
tated to blackmail me if I'd compromised myself with his
wife? Not he.

SIR PATRICK. Dont waste your time wrangling over
him. A blackguard's a blackguard; an honest man's an honest man; and neither of them will ever be at a loss for a
religion or a morality to prove that their ways are the right
ways. It's the same with nations, the same with professions,
the same all the world over and always will be.

B. B. Ah, well, perhaps, perhaps, perhaps. Still, d e
m o r t u i s   n i l   n i s i   b o n u m. He died extremely
well, remarkably well. He has set us an example: let us en-
deavor to follow it rather than harp on the weaknesses that
have perished with him. I think it is Shakespear who says
that the good that most men do lives after them: the evil lies
interréd with their bones. Yes: interréd with their bones.
Believe me, Paddy, we are all mortal. It is the common
lot, Ridgeon. Say what you will, Walpole, Nature's debt
must be paid. If tis not to-day, twill be to-morrow.

THE DOCTOR'S DILEMMA
To-morrow and to-morrow and to-morrow
After life's fitful fever they sleep well
And like this insubstantial bourne from which
No traveller returns
Leave not a wrack behind.

Walpole is about to speak, but B. B., suddenly and vehemently proceeding, extinguishes him.

Out, out, brief candle:
For nothing canst thou to damnation add
The readiness is all.

WALPOLE [*gently; for B. B.'s feeling, absurdly expressed as it is, is too sincere and humane to be ridiculed*] Yes, B. B. Death makes people go on like that. I dont know why it should; but it does. By the way, what are we going to do? Ought we to clear out; or had we better wait and see whether Mrs Dubedat will come back?

SIR PATRICK. I think we'd better go. We can tell the charwoman what to do.

They take their hats and go to the door.

MRS DUBEDAT [*coming from the inner door wonderfully and beautifully dressed, and radiant, carrying a great piece of purple silk, handsomely embroidered, over her arm*] I'm so sorry to have kept you waiting.

SIR PATRICK		Dont mention it, madam.
B. B.	[*amazed, all together in a confused murmur*]	Not at all, not at all.
RIDGEON		By no means.
WALPOLE		It doesnt matter in the least.

MRS DUBEDAT [*coming to them*] I felt that I must shake hands with his friends once before we part to-day. We have shared together a great privilege and a great happiness. I dont think we can ever think of ourselves as ordinary people again. We have had a wonderful experience; and that gives us a common faith, a common ideal, that nobody else can quite have. Life will always be beautiful to us: death will always be beautiful to us. May we shake hands on that?

SIR PATRICK [*shaking hands*] Remember: all letters had better be left to your solicitor. Let him open everything and settle everything. Thats the law, you know.

MRS DUBEDAT. Oh, thank you: I didnt know. [*Sir Patrick goes*].

WALPOLE. Good-bye. I blame myself: I should have insisted on operating. [*He goes*].

B. B. I will send the proper people: they will know what to do: you shall have no trouble. G o o d-bye, my dear lady. [*He goes*].

RIDGEON. Good-bye. [*He offers his hand*].

MRS DUBEDAT [*drawing back with gentle majesty*] I said his f r i e n d s, Sir Colenso. [*He bows and goes*].

She unfolds the great piece of silk, and goes into the recess to cover her dead.

ACT V

ONE of the smaller Bond Street Picture Galleries. The entrance is from a picture shop. Nearly in the middle of the gallery there is a writing-table; at which the Secretary, fashionably dressed, sits with his back to the entrance, correcting catalogue proofs. Some copies of a new book are on the desk, also the Secretary's shining hat and a couple of magnifying glasses. At the side, on his left, a little behind him, is a small door marked PRIVATE. Near the same side is a cushioned bench parallel to the walls, which are covered with Dubedat's works. Two screens, also covered with drawings, stand near the corners right and left of the entrance.

Jennifer, beautifully dressed and apparently very happy and prosperous, comes into the gallery through the private door.

JENNIFER. Have the catalogues come yet, Mr Danby?

THE SECRETARY. Not yet.

JENNIFER. What a shame! It's a quarter past: the private view will begin in less than half an hour.

THE SECRETARY. I think I'd better run over to the printers to hurry them up.

JENNIFER. Oh, if you would be so good, Mr Danby. I'll take your place while youre away.

THE SECRETARY. If anyone should come before the time dont take any notice. The commissionaire wont let anyone through unless he knows him. We have a few people who like to come before the crowd—people who really buy; and of course we're glad to see them. Have you seen the notices in Brush and Crayon and in The Easel?

JENNIFER [indignantly] Yes: most disgraceful. They write quite patronizingly, as if they were Mr Dubedat's superiors. After all the cigars and sandwiches they had from us on the press day, and all they drank, I really think it is infamous that they should write like that. I hope you have not sent them tickets for to-day.

179

THE DOCTOR'S DILEMMA

THE SECRETARY. Oh, they wont come again: theres no lunch to-day. The advance copies of your book have come. [*He indicates the new books*].

JENNIFER [*pouncing on a copy, wildly excited*] Give it to me. Oh! excuse me a moment [*she runs away with it through the private door*].

The Secretary takes a mirror from his drawer and smartens himself before going out. Ridgeon comes in.

RIDGEON. Good morning. May I look round, as usual, before the doors open?

THE SECRETARY. Certainly, Sir Colenso. I'm sorry the catalogues have not come: I'm just going to see about them. Heres my own list, if you dont mind.

RIDGEON. Thanks. Whats this? [*He takes up one of the new books*].

THE SECRETARY. Thats just come in. An advance copy of Mrs Dubedat's Life of her late husband.

RIDGEON [*reading the title*] The Story of a King of Men. By His Wife. [*He looks at the portrait frontispiece*]. Ay: there he is. You knew him here, I suppose.

THE SECRETARY. Oh, we knew him. Better than she did, Sir Colenso, in some ways, perhaps.

RIDGEON. So did I. [*They look significantly at one another*]. I'll take a look round.

The Secretary puts on the shining hat and goes out. Ridgeon begins looking at the pictures. Presently he comes back to the table for a magnifying glass, and scrutinizes a drawing very closely. He sighs; shakes his head, as if constrained to admit the extraordinary fascination and merit of the work; then marks the Secretary's list. Proceeding with his survey, he disappears behind the screen. Jennifer comes back with her book. A look round satisfies her that she is alone. She seats herself at the table and admires the memoir—her first printed book—to her heart's content. Ridgeon re-appears, face to the wall, scrutinizing the drawings. After using his glass again, he steps back to get a more distant view of one of the larger pictures. She hastily closes

180

Photo by Vandamm Studio

Jennifer [innocently surprised] "In lo— You! An elderly man!"

Katharine Cornell and Raymond Massey

THE DOCTOR'S DILEMMA

the book at the sound; looks round; recognizes him; and stares, petrified. He takes a further step back which brings him nearer to her.

RIDGEON [*shaking his head as before, ejaculates*] Clever brute! [*She flushes as though he had struck her. He turns to put the glass down on the desk, and finds himself face to face with her intent gaze*]. I beg your pardon. I thought I was alone.

JENNIFER [*controlling herself, and speaking steadily and meaningly*] I am glad we have met, Sir Colenso Ridgeon. I met Dr Blenkinsop yesterday. I congratulate you on a wonderful cure.

RIDGEON [*can find no words: makes an embarrassed gesture of assent after a moment's silence, and puts down the glass and the Secretary's list on the table*].

JENNIFER. He looked the picture of health and strength and prosperity. [*She looks for a moment at the walls, contrasting Blenkinsop's fortune with the artist's fate*].

RIDGEON [*in low tones, still embarrassed*] He has been fortunate.

JENNIFER. V e r y fortunate. His life has been spared.

RIDGEON. I mean that he has been made a Medical Officer of Health. He cured the Chairman of the Borough Council very successfully.

JENNIFER. With y o u r medicines?

RIDGEON. No. I believe it was with a pound of ripe greengages.

JENNIFER [*with deep gravity*] Funny!

RIDGEON. Yes. Life does not cease to be funny when people die any more than it ceases to be serious when people laugh.

JENNIFER. Dr Blenkinsop said one very strange thing to me.

RIDGEON. What was that?

JENNIFER. He said that private practice in medicine ought to be put down by law. When I asked him why, he said that private doctors were ignorant licensed murderers.

181

RIDGEON. That is what the public doctor always thinks of the private doctor. Well, Blenkinsop ought to know. He was a private doctor long enough himself. Come! you have talked at me long enough. Talk to me. You have something to reproach me with. There is reproach in your face, in your voice: you are full of it. Out with it.

JENNIFER. It is too late for reproaches now. When I turned and saw you just now, I wondered how you could come here coolly to look at his pictures. You answered the question. To you, he was only a clever brute.

RIDGEON [*quivering*] Oh, dont. You know I did not know you were here.

JENNIFER [*raising her head a little with a quite gentle impulse of pride*] You think it only mattered because I heard it. As if it could touch me, or touch him! Dont you see that what is really wonderful is that to you living things have no souls.

RIDGEON [*with a sceptical shrug*] The soul is an organ I have not come across in the course of my anatomical work.

JENNIFER. You know you would not dare to say such a silly thing as that to anybody but a woman whose mind you despise. If you dissected me you could not find my conscience. Do you think I have got none?

RIDGEON. I have met people who had none.

JENNIFER. Clever brutes? Do you know, doctor, that some of the dearest and most faithful friends I ever had were only brutes! You would have vivisected them. The dearest and greatest of all my friends had a sort of beauty and affectionateness that only animals have. I hope you may never feel what I felt when I had to put him into the hands of men who defend the torture of animals because they are only brutes.

RIDGEON. Well, did you find us so very cruel, after all? They tell me that though you have dropped me, you stay for weeks with the Bloomfield Boningtons and the Walpoles. I think it must be true, because they never mention you to me now.

THE DOCTOR'S DILEMMA

JENNIFER. The animals in Sir Ralph's house are like spoiled children. When Mr Walpole had to take a splinter out of the mastiff's paw, I had to hold the poor dog myself; and Mr Walpole had to turn Sir Ralph out of the room. And Mrs Walpole has to tell the gardener not to kill wasps when Mr Walpole is looking. But there are doctors who are naturally cruel; and there are others who get used to cruelty and are callous about it. They blind themselves to the souls of animals; and that blinds them to the souls of men and women. You made a dreadful mistake about Louis; but you would not have made it if you had not trained yourself to make the same mistake about dogs. You saw nothing in them but dumb brutes; and so you could see nothing in him but a clever brute.

RIDGEON [*with sudden resolution*] I made no mistake whatever about him.

JENNIFER. Oh, doctor!

RIDGEON [*obstinately*] I made no mistake whatever about him.

JENNIFER. Have you forgotten that he died?

RIDGEON [*with a sweep of his hand towards the pictures*] He is not dead. He is there. [*Taking up the book*] And there.

JENNIFER. [*springing up with blazing eyes*] Put that down. How dare you touch it?

Ridgeon, amazed at the fierceness of the outburst, puts it down with a deprecatory shrug. She takes it up and looks at it as if he had profaned a relic.

RIDGEON. I am very sorry. I see I had better go.

JENNIFER [*putting the book down*] I beg your pardon. I—I forgot myself. But it is not yet—it is a private copy.

RIDGEON. But for me it would have been a very different book.

JENNIFER. But for you it would have been a longer one.

RIDGEON. You know then that I killed him?

JENNIFER [*suddenly moved and softened*] Oh, doctor, if you acknowledge that—if you have confessed it to yourself—if you realize what you have done, then there is forgiveness. I trusted in your strength instinctively at first; then I thought I had mistaken callousness for strength. Can you blame me? But if it was really strength—if it was only such a mistake as we all make sometimes—it will make me so happy to be friends with you again.

RIDGEON. I tell you I made no mistake. I cured Blenkinsop: was there any mistake there?

JENNIFER. He recovered. Oh, dont be foolishly proud, doctor. Confess to a failure, and save our friendship. Remember, Sir Ralph gave Louis your medicine; and it made him worse.

RIDGEON. I cant be your friend on false pretences. Something has got me by the throat: the truth must come out. I used that medicine myself on Blenkinsop. It did not make him worse. It is a dangerous medicine: it cured Blenkinsop: it killed Louis Dubedat. When I handle it, it cures. When another man handles it, it kills—sometimes.

JENNIFER [*naïvely: not yet taking it all in*] Then why did you let Sir Ralph give it to Louis?

RIDGEON. I'm going to tell you. I did it because I was in love with you.

JENNIFER [*innocently surprised*] In lo— You! an elderly man!

RIDGEON [*thunderstruck, raising his fists to heaven*] Dubedat: thou art avenged! [*He drops his hands and collapses on the bench*]. I never thought of that. I suppose I appear to you a ridiculous old fogey.

JENNIFER. But surely—I did not mean to offend you, indeed—but you must be at least twenty years older than I am.

RIDGEON. Oh, quite. More, perhaps. In twenty years you will understand how little difference that makes.

JENNIFER. But even so, how could you think that I— his wife—could ever think of y o u—

RIDGEON [*stopping her with a nervous waving of his*

fingers] Yes, yes, yes, yes: I quite understand: you neednt rub it in.

JENNIFER. But—oh, it is only dawning on me now—I was so surprised at first—do you dare to tell me that it was to gratify a miserable jealousy that you deliberately—oh! oh! you murdered him.

RIDGEON. I think I did. It really comes to that.

> Thou shalt not kill, but needst not strive
> Officiously to keep alive.

I suppose—yes: I killed him.

JENNIFER. And you tell me that! to my face! callously! You are not afraid!

RIDGEON. I am a doctor: I have nothing to fear. It is not an indictable offence to call in B. B. Perhaps it ought to be; but it isnt.

JENNIFER. I did not mean that. I meant afraid of my taking the law into my own hands, and killing you.

RIDGEON. I am so hopelessly idiotic about you that I should not mind it a bit. You would always remember me if you did that.

JENNIFER. I shall remember you always as a little man who tried to kill a great one.

RIDGEON. Pardon me. I succeeded.

JENNIFER [*with quiet conviction*] No. Doctors think they hold the keys of life and death; but it is not their will that is fulfilled. I dont believe you made any difference at all.

RIDGEON. Perhaps not. But I intended to.

JENNIFER [*looking at him amazedly: not without pity*] And you tried to destroy that wonderful and beautiful life merely because you grudged him a woman whom you could never have expected to care for you!

RIDGEON. Who kissed my hands. Who believed in me. Who told me her friendship lasted until death.

JENNIFER. And whom you were betraying.

185

THE DOCTOR'S DILEMMA

RIDGEON. No. Whom I was saving.

JENNIFER [*gently*] Pray, doctor, from what?

RIDGEON. From making a terrible discovery. From having your life laid waste.

JENNIFER. How?

RIDGEON. No matter. I h a v e saved you. I have been the best friend you ever had. You are happy. You are well. His works are an imperishable joy and pride for you.

JENNIFER. And you think that is y o u r doing. Oh doctor, doctor! Sir Patrick is right: you do think you are a little god. How can you be so silly? Y o u did not paint those pictures which are my imperishable joy and pride: y o u did not speak the words that will always be heavenly music in my ears. I listen to them now whenever I am tired or sad. That is why I am always happy.

RIDGEON. Yes, now that he is dead. Were you always happy when he was alive?

JENNIFER [*wounded*] Oh, you are cruel, cruel. When he was alive I did not know the greatness of my blessing. I worried meanly about little things. I was unkind to him. I was unworthy of him.

RIDGEON [*laughing bitterly*] Ha!

JENNIFER. Dont insult me: dont blaspheme. [*She snatches up the book and presses it to her heart in a paroxysm of remorse, exclaiming*] Oh, my King of Men!

RIDGEON. King of Men! Oh, this is too monstrous, too grotesque. We cruel doctors have kept the secret from you faithfully; but it is like all secrets: it will not keep itself. The buried truth germinates and breaks through to the light.

JENNIFER. What truth?

RIDGEON. What truth! Why, that Louis Dubedat, King of Men, was the most entire and perfect scoundrel, the most miraculously mean rascal, the most callously selfish blackguard that ever made a wife miserable.

JENNIFER [*unshaken: calm and lovely*] He made his wife the happiest woman in the world, doctor.

186

THE DOCTOR'S DILEMMA

RIDGEON. No: by all thats true on earth, he made his w i d o w the happiest woman in the world; but it was I who made her a widow. And her happiness is my justification and my reward. Now you know what I did and what I thought of him. Be as angry with me as you like: at least you know me as I really am. If you ever come to care for an elderly man, you will know what you are caring for.

JENNIFER [*kind and quiet*] I am not angry with you any more, Sir Colenso. I knew quite well that you did not like Louis; but it is not your fault: you dont understand: that is all. You never could have believed in him. It is just like your not believing in my religion: it is a sort of sixth sense that you have not got. And [*with a gentle reassuring movement towards him*] dont think that you have shocked me so dreadfully. I know quite well what you mean by his selfishness. He sacrificed everything for his art. In a certain sense he had even to sacrifice everybody—

RIDGEON. Everybody except himself. By keeping that back he lost the right to sacrifice you, and gave me the right to sacrifice him. Which I did.

JENNIFER [*shaking her head, pitying his error*] He was one of the men who know what women know: that self-sacrifice is vain and cowardly.

RIDGEON. Yes, when the sacrifice is rejected and thrown away. Not when it becomes the food of godhead.

JENNIFER. I dont understand that. And I cant argue with you: you are clever enough to puzzle me, but not to shake me. You are so utterly, so wildly wrong; so incapable of appreciating Louis—

RIDGEON. Oh! [*taking up the Secretary's list*] I have marked five pictures as sold to me.

JENNIFER. They will not be sold to you. Louis' creditors insisted on selling them; but this is my birthday; and they were all bought in for me this morning by my husband.

RIDGEON. By whom? ! ! !

JENNIFER. By my husband.

RIDGEON [*gabbling and stuttering*] What husband?

187

Whose husband? Which husband? Whom? how? what?
Do you mean to say that you have married again?

JENNIFER. Do you forget that Louis disliked widows,
and that people who have married happily once always
marry again?

RIDGEON. Then I have committed a purely disinterested
murder!

The Secretary returns with a pile of catalogues.

THE SECRETARY. Just got the first batch of catalogues
in time. The doors are open.

JENNIFER [*to Ridgeon, politely*] So glad you like the
pictures, Sir Colenso. Good morning.

RIDGEON. Good morning. [*He goes towards the door;
hesitates; turns to say something more; gives it up as a bad
job; and goes*].

Date Due